MW00378984

Newman's Wave

A story by Michael Sullivan

Chapter 1

Just off Pleasure Point, a surfing mecca in Santa
Cruz, California, two young men
 sat on their boards, well beyond the line of anxious
surfers waiting for just the right wave, staring out
toward the sea. Neither said a word to the other. One
had removed the cap to his wetsuit. Around his neck,
one wore a lanyard with a small plastic bottle attached
to it. He wanted to feel and hear in the moment. The
off shore breeze had his shoulder length hair looking
something like Medusa. The spray coming off an
occasional backwash, a wave returning to the ocean
that collides with an incoming wave, stung his face
like tiny needles. He closed his eyes, counting the
seconds between the waves as they crashed against
the shore. It sounded like the clash of the giant
symbols in a symphony. He savored the smell of the
piles of seaweed scattered along the shore. The gray
clouds of early morning acted as a harbinger of a
miserable day, but those devoted to surfing knew
within a few hours the sun would break through and
bring new life to the drab color of the ocean water and
the surrounding cliffs fully exposed by the low tide.

"Do you think today will be the day?" Fletcher asked.

"We'll see," answered Danny, as he turned to check out the next set of waves.

Glancing toward shore, Danny Archer could see the earliest spectators arrive. Between the O'Neil House, named after the legendary surf board designer, Jack O'Neil, four short blocks north of Elizabeth's Market, they began to take their places along the rail fence that lined the edge of the cliff. Others sat on wooden benches conveniently staged along East Cliff Drive. Some had stopped at Elizabeth's Market for a morning coffee. Others had their own travel mugs, some filled with pure java, others laced with a touch of Irish Whiskey.

As he scanned the cliff side, he marveled how the color of the concrete poured over the cliff side by the Coastal Commission to prevent erosion changed with the emerging sun. When protected by cloud cover, the concrete blended in with the brownish sand at its base to look like some weird nondescript sculpture running the length of East Cliff Drive. When exposed to the emerging rays of the sun, the concrete seemed to absorb the aqua green color of the ocean. The movement of clouds created a virtual kaleidoscope of colors to the surfer willing to take the time to look.

Danny Archer's mind was hardly focusing on the landscape. He was remembering the years following his father's death; problems with his mother, trouble at school and with the police. The expulsion issue at Burke Preparatory was the worst. His was anything but an idyllic childhood. His mother did the best she could. Lucky for her, there was Newman.

****

Two things told him it was time to paddle in; hunger pangs causing his stomach to growl, and the diminutive waves. Those gentle rollers that pandered to beginning surfers were not the kind he wanted to honor his friend.

"Let's go, Fletch," Danny said to his friend, who obediently complied and started paddling toward shore.

At the top of the steps, the two young men paused to take one more look at the surf. Danny looked off to his left at the empty bench behind him. *Why him?* Danny thought. The man he called Newman had always been there, no matter what day of the week it was or what time it was. He would sit there with a large writing pad in his lap, sometimes writing for minutes on end, and other times staring out at the waves and surfers. Newman never failed to ask Danny and Fletch, "How's the surf?" and when they responded "great," he would smile, stretch his arms upward, then clasp his hands behind his head and say, "As it should be." Sometimes their response was, "It sucked." He would look at them, smile, stretch his arms upward, then clasp his hands behind his head and reply, "It won't tomorrow."

These simple words of encouragement were not what Danny missed most. It was how the old man listened to him, how he answered Danny's questions or responded to problems the boy was having. But

4

always, he would end up talking about the surf. Danny smiled to himself as he remembered his first encounter with the old man.

****

His name was Newman. That's how everyone knew him. No first name, just Newman. He could be found almost any day sitting in a folding chair, positioned near the steps next to Jack O'Neil's house where 36th avenue runs into East Cliff Drive. For years, he had been a fixture there. Anyone who spent any length of time surfing Pleasure Point knew Newman.

****

It was a Chamber of Commerce day in Santa Cruz, California—not a cloud in the sky, water like glass, and Newman was soaking it all in. His notebook lay open on his lap. His mind was searching for an introduction to the next paragraph in his story when the impassioned voice of a woman standing a few feet away caught his attention. He listened to the woman giving cautious instructions to her son.

"Danny, you've got to be careful. Please don't go out too far," she pleaded.

The pre-adolescent teenager gave her an exasperated 'Whatever' shrug of his shoulders. This only irritated his mother more. *Must be approaching teenage years*, Newman thought.

"Now you listen to me, Danny Archer," she said, taking hold of his shoulder, "I am your mother."

Getting his attention in a way that only served to embarrass him, the boy answered, "I know Mom, I'll be careful. I'm just going to float on my board."

A smiled formed on Newman's face, as the mother knelt down and kissed her son on the top of his head.

"Have fun then," she said. She watched as her son struggled to balance his small surfboard as he walked down the steps to the sand. She stood next to the rail fence, a death grip on the top rail. Tears were freely flowing down her face.

"Worried about him?" Newman asked.

She could only nod. Her lungs seemed to suck in air to control her breathing. The boy zipped up his wetsuit, then guided his crozier flextail surf board into the shallow water. He straddled the board and sat there. The waves broke so far out at low tide, there were about 40 yards of gentle shifting water for the boy to idle in. For the better part of an hour, the boy sat on his board staring out to the breaking waves.

"Pardon me for asking," Newman inquired, "but is your son ok?"

She released her grip on the fence to wipe away her tears with a handkerchief.

"His father died a year ago," she said. "Danny adored him. Now, all he wants to do is sit on his surfboard and stare out at the waves. It's as if he's looking for his father."

"Did his father like to surf?" Newman asked.

"Like? My God, he loved it," the woman responded. "Whenever he could, he'd be down here at sun up to get as much surfing in as he could before he went to work."

A man after my own heart, Newman thought.

"I've taught a lot of kids to surf. Would you mind if I talked to him?" Newman asked.

"Please," she said, though her eyes said much more; *help him to be himself.*

Newman walked across the street to where his truck was parked on the corner of 36th avenue. He changed into his wetsuit, grabbed his board, headed back across the street and walked down the stairs to the sand. He stood near the water's edge, holding his board on end, not twenty feet from the boy. Newman set his board in the water and walked out to the boy.

"Hi Danny. My name's Newman. Are you headed out?" he asked.

Danny turned to him, bewildered that a stranger would know his name.

Sensing the boy's confusion, Newman said, "I was talking with your mom." He pointed up to the fence that lined the cliffs. "She said I could talk to you."

Danny looked up to the top of the cliffs. His mother smiled and gave him a wave.

So Newman repeated his question, "Are you headed out?"

Danny shook his head 'No'. "I'm not good enough."

"Would you like to go out?" Newman asked, knowing that the waves were nothing but ankle busters, a term for very small rolling waves.

Debbie had come down to the shore, hoping to sneak in on the conversation between her son and the stranger, Newman. She waded out until she was about knee deep, and right behind the two.

"I have to ask my Mom," Danny said.

"Asked me what, Danny?" she said.

The boy looked at his mother. "This man..." He'd forgotten his name.

Newman smiled. "My name's Newman."

"Oh yeah. Newman asked me if I wanted to go out with him. Can I, Mom?"

She had boxed herself into a corner and she knew it. *No going back now,* she thought.

"Danny, if you want to, I'm sure Mr. Newman could teach you a few things, that is if you don't mind?" she said, glancing at Newman.

The boy practically fell off his board at the sound of his mom's voice.

"Are you sure, Mom?" a smile beaming over her son's face.

"It's up to Mr. Newman, Danny." She nearly choked on her words. It had been months since she had seen her son smile.

"It's plain Newman, Debbie, and yes, I've love to take Danny out," Newman replied.

With an approving smile from his mother, Danny shouted, "Let's go, Mr. Newman."

"Then hop on, Danny. We'll go out on my board for the first couple of times. And remember, it's Newman, just plain Newman."

With that, Danny got off his small board, shoved it toward his mother, then hopped on Newman's board. The ten foot Bing had ample room for the two. Debbie took Danny's board to shore, then climbed to a large flat area on the rocks near the stairs, and watched.

For the next few hours, Debbie watched as Newman paddled his board through the gentle waves with Danny, sitting in front at first, then lying down and paddling at Newman's commands. They sat just outside where the waves started to curl.

"First things first, Danny," Newman said. "The waves will break to your right. You want to make sure you never go straight toward the shore. Always keep the wave close to your right shoulder. Got it?"

Danny nodded as if he did, but in truth, he wasn't sure. Only experience would drive home Newman's words. Newman paddled his way toward shore. When they got to shallow waters, he stopped and turned his board seaward.

"See those three guys taking that wave?" Newman asked, pointing to three surfers paddling as fast as they could.

"Yeah," replied Danny.

"The one farthest to the right has the right of way, so to speak. Now if you're out there, the surfer farthest to your left has the right of way. Know that what means?"

Danny shook his head.

"If you take a wave and someone to your left takes the same wave, unless there's a lot of room between you two, peel off and let the person to your left take the wave."

"But what if it's a really good wave?" Danny rebutted.

"Doesn't matter, Danny. It's the right thing to do. It's the respect one surfer gives another."

The lesson continued as Newman explained where waves break at low tide and high tide.

"If you ever decide to surf at a higher tide, you be careful," Newman cautioned the boy. "Waves break closest to shore at high tide. Waves are harder to catch when they break close to shore."

Debbie pulled her knees to her breast as a sudden chill came over her. It should be his father teaching him, not some stranger. She lowered her head and let the tears flow. When Newman and Danny finally returned to shore, the boy ran to his mother, who was sitting on a large flat rock formation at the base of the steps.

"Mom, that was great," shouted an enthusiastic Danny. "I learned a bunch of stuff."

"He's a quick learner," Newman said, patting the boy on his head.

"He's a lot like his father," Debbie replied.

Danny turned to Newman. "Do you think we could do this again, Newman?"

"Let me tell you something about surfing, Danny. It can make you feel alive, like living on the edge. It can also be deadly. People have died in surfing accidents."

His words seemed lost on the boy. "But when can we do this again?" he repeated.

"When the time's right," Newman replied.

Confusion spread over Danny's face. *When isn't the time right to go surfing?* he thought. "When's that?" the boy asked.

"When you're done with your chores around the house, got your homework done, and anything else your mom needs help with," Newman said.

And anything else she needs help with was like an avalanche about to bury the boy. Newman felt for the boy.

"Look, Danny," Newman continued. "Everybody out there," he said, pointing to the surfers, "had to get something done in order to have the time to surf. Now, when your Mom gives you the okay, I'll be waiting."

Debbie smiled as Danny grabbed hold of his board. The mention of his father gave Danny a renewed sense of determination and hope as he and his mom headed home.

****

Newman watched mother and son head home. He wondered how a boy like Danny would have made it in the Santa Cruz of old, the Santa Cruz Newman knew. In the fifties, Santa Cruz was this sleepy little coastal town that lay virtually dormant for nine months of the year. The locals had their run of the best surfing spots in the area. A multitude of Ford and Mercury "Woodies" dominated the parking spots near the beach. But with the coming of summer, vacationers poured into the coastal town, and with that came crowded beaches, and more surfers to compete for the waves to which the locals had previously had exclusive access. Old timers took the inconvenience of the increased population with a grain of salt, except for two weekends during the summer; Fourth of July weekend and Labor Day weekend. On those two weekends, hordes of college kids descended into Santa Cruz, crowding as many bodies as they could into every available motel room. Their sole purpose was to stay as drunk as they could, meet and lay as many co-eds as possible, and fight with whomever would insult their treasured fraternity or college.

By the end of the sixties, things had changed. First came the University of California at Santa Cruz (UCSC) in 1965. Newman had predicted a cultural revolution, and he was right. Aside from soaring property values, a new level of intelligentsia emerged. The university administration was more focused on teaching students to question rather than remember. As a result, like college and university campuses across the nation, UCSC had its share of student protests over numerous university policies. Sometimes, it seemed students protested just to protest.

The university wasn't the students' only target. The moral conscience of America was being poked and prodded to rise up against the war in Vietnam. Those opposed to the war were particularly effective in getting on prime time news channels by staging marches on Highway 17 coming into Santa Cruz from the south bay and on Highway 1 north and south of Santa Cruz on weekends. Between the protesters, those protesting the protesters, and the curious bystanders, Santa Cruz was developing a reputation its founding fathers never anticipated.

If protests against the university and the war in Vietnam weren't enough, the passage of the Civil Rights Act of 1964 added fuel to the fire for social change. The only thing whiter than the sand on Santa Cruz beaches was its population. The infusion of a multi-ethnic student body into the local populace was tough to take for some. The emergence of the "Hippie Culture" seemed to go hand in hand with the war protesters, and now marches for civil rights equality forced the home grown folks of Santa Cruz to see up front and personal the rage that came from decades of racial discrimination and inequality. No longer were protest marches something taking place in other cities. The citizens had front row seats to watch in their own backyard.

A different place for a mother to raise her child, Newman thought. Navigating adolescence was difficult at best. To do it with these social dynamics surrounding you made the difficult seem impossible.

****

Chapter 2

For Danny Archer and his mother, Debbie, home was a small two-bedroom forties style house at 529 36th avenue. Danny's room was in the back of the house with an exit to the back yard. But his favorite place was a loft above his bedroom. It was his special place when he needed to get away from whatever twelve-year old boys want to get away from. Running off Portola Drive, 36th avenue was two blocks long and led to the closest access point to the water off Pleasure Point. At irregular intervals, towering palm trees rose on both sides of the street. Acting like weather vanes, their dangling fronds would indicate the direction of the wind. If an onshore wind swayed the fronds inland, the surf would not be good. When an off shore wind swayed the fronds toward the ocean, the surf tended to be better.

Living there was both a blessing and a curse. If you loved to surf, you could not be in a better location. Unfortunately, surfers used every bit of available street side parking, including, at times, blocking private driveways. Shortly after sunrise, they would arrive in every type of vehicle imaginable, from SUVs to sedans to the quintessential Santa Cruz homemade camper made out of cedar shingles framed on the back of a twenty-something year old pickup truck. The ritual was the same whether you were a newbie or an old timer. A courteous greeting of, "Looks like a great day for waves," was exchanged by everyone. Then the wet suits came out. Every surf board was examined for just the right amount of wax, then, one by one, surfers walked down the street to East Cliff Drive and the cement stairs leading to the water. An occasional home owner would be having coffee in the front yard and casually wave to the parade of surfers passing by. In addition to those lucky enough to find a parking spot, others rode bicycles fitted with special racks for carrying a surfboard. Others just carried their boards under their arm. All were headed in search of the perfect wave.

Thirty Sixth avenue was lined with homes as different as the people who lived in Santa Cruz. There were the fifties style bungalows whose garages, in most cases, had been converted into another room so the landlord could generate the maximum rental income. Craftsman homes of the same vintage often butted up to each other utilizing every inch of land available. Every so often someone who had smoked one too many joints of 'Panama Gold' built a house whose design model must have faded in and out of consciousness during construction, like the one with dark shingles, bright red trimmed windows lined with a glass wind shield, Chinese style eaves and a roof top patio with the latest umbrella table and chairs from Home Depot.

****

He had finished the last of his Pete's coffee and turned to toss the empty cup in the trash can when he saw two boys headed toward him. *His work must be done,* thought a smiling Newman. It was a little past three in the afternoon, and the boys would have an hour or so of good surf before the incoming tide would make surfing too dangerous.

"Hi, Newman," Danny called out. "How's the surf?"

"Three footers, pretty nice lines. Should be a good day," Newman said.

"Newman, this is my friend Fletcher. Fletcher, this is my friend, Newman," Danny said by way of introduction.

The two shook hands.

"You surf much, Fletcher?" Newman asked.

"Yes sir," Danny's friend answered, "I'm almost as good as Danny."

Newman smiled at the boy's manners, something clearly missing in many of the young people Newman came into contact with.

"He'll be able to teach you a few things," Newman said.

"You will show him, won't you, Danny?" Newman said, the question being totally unnecessary.

Danny kept his eyes on the surf, preferring not to respond to the old man's question. He was remembering an old lesson he learned from him, *Watch the waves.*

"Sure I will," Danny replied. "Let's go Fletch. Just follow my lead and you'll be ok."

Newman watched as each boy attached the surf board's leash to his ankle and then paddled through the breaking surf to a point where twenty or so surfers sat waiting for the next set to start. As he watched the boys approach the line of surfers, something happened that bothered him. A surfer who had waited patiently for just the right wave began to paddle. He had positioned himself perfectly, right where the curl of the wave starts. He rose to his feet when suddenly a second surfer near him took off. To avoid a collision, the first surfer had to peel quickly to his left, while the surfer who had "dropped in" continued down the line of the wave. In doing so, he lost his balance and fell into the breaking wave. *Asshole,* Newman thought as he peered through his binoculars. The fallen surfer had retrieved his board and paddled back to join the others.

Newman shifted his focus to the hotdog surfer. The nine-foot bright blue 'Stormblade' was easy to spot. When its rider finished his run, he shifted his board seaward and headed back to the pack. This wasn't the first time Newman had seen the aggressive surfer strut his stuff. Over the last few weeks, Newman had seen him cut off any number of surfers trying to catch a wave. On two occasions, the "Aggro," an Australian expression for an aggressive surfer, as Newman called him, had actually collided with another surfer. One time, his victim waited on the beach for the "Aggro" to come ashore. Newman had been there that day and he eagerly waited for the opportunity to see the "Aggro" get his comeuppance.

He would be disappointed. After seeing the surfer on shore flash him the middle finger, the "Aggro" paddled off toward Capitola.

Not bad. Not bad at all, Newman thought, keeping his binoculars focused on his two new friends. He followed them through a couple of small sets. Danny had learned well from the few lessons Newman had given him. The last wave of a small set began to form and Newman could see Danny's friend Fletcher begin to paddle. He caught it perfectly, getting to his feet with more agility than Newman would have given him credit for. That's when Newman noticed the blue 'Stormblade' come slicing down the face of the wave to the right of Danny's friend. He wasn't going to give the kid a break. He turned a hard right, but not before smacking into the kid, who flew into the air along with his board.

Newman was on his feet, adjusting the binoculars to see exactly where the kid would come up. He sighed a sigh of relief when he saw Fletcher pulling himself onto his board. Then Newman noticed the bloody nose on the kid. It took him a few minutes for Newman to get into his wetsuit and get his board to the edge of the water. For Newman, the idiot on the blue 'Stormblade' was as bad as a drunk driver and Newman was going to play cop. With both arms simultaneously making long deep pulls into the water, Newman paddled out to the Fletcher.

"Are you ok, Buddy?"

The kid nodded yes, but Newman couldn't help but notice the tears in his eyes.

"Head to shore," he said, "there's a towel in my gym bag next to my chair. You can use it."

Newman looked to find the blue 'Stormblade'. The clown was sitting on his board not five feet from Fletcher's friend, Danny. Newman paddled hard to catch him before he caught another wave.

"Hi, Newman. Didn't know you could surf!" Danny called out, as Newman approached him.

"Yeah, I know a little," Newman responded, paddling over to 'Stormblade'.

"A little aggressive out here, aren't you?"

"You talking to me?" the rider scoffed.

"As a matter of fact, I am," Newman replied.

"And you care because?" the surfer sounded, the challenge in his voice was obvious.

Newman smirked. *Well, you don't leave me much choice.* "I care because I choose to. There's enough danger out here without some asshole like you putting someone's life in jeopardy so…" reaching out with his right arm, he grabbed the surfer by his left shoulder, jerked him off his board and slammed him across his own board. "You ever cut someone off like that again, you'll swim to shore because I will break that board over your god damn head! You get me?"

Unable to answer because he was still trying to get his breath, the hot shot surfer could only nod his head.

"Good," Newman answered, letting him slide off his board and into the water.

Back at his spot on the cliff, Newman attended to Fletcher's bloody nose, which by now was clotting nicely. Danny watched attentively. When he was done, Newman said, "You didn't do too bad out there today."

Fletcher smiled, along with Danny.

"You do that very often?" Danny asked, pointing to the rider on the blue 'Stormblade' who was climbing up the cement stairs.

"No, I don't," Newman answered. "I try to avoid those kinds of confrontations at all cost, but sometimes you can't avoid them."

Wiping his face with a towel, Newman said, "Needlessly hurting someone has no place in surfing."

"Do you think anything will happen after what you did?"

"Maybe," Newman said. "Sometimes doing the right thing has consequences, Danny, just like doing the wrong thing. You still need to do the right thing."

As the boys headed back to Danny's house, Fletcher said, "I think I found a new friend."

Danny glanced back over his shoulder. "I think you did."

****

He peeled off his wetsuit, hanging it over the backyard fence, then jumped under the outdoor shower. His mom leaned forward to the opened kitchen window over the sink and called out, "Good day, Danny?"

"Any day surfing is a good day, Mom," he replied.

Debbie Archer smiled, fighting back the tears. Her husband used to say the same thing whenever he returned from surfing. It had been nearly three years since he died in a construction accident, and not a day went by that the pain of his memory didn't tear her heart in two.

Daniel Archer Sr., "Big Dan" as he was called by his crew, worked for a construction company that specialized in erecting metal buildings. One time, Debbie had driven by his work site to drop off a hot lunch. She almost threw up when she saw him walking the top place of a wall nearly 30 feet high. "Big Dan" had an incredible sense of balance and was absolutely fearless when it came to heights. Debbie had begged him to be careful. "I don't know what I'd do if you ever fell," she pleaded. "It's not the fall you have to worry about, Babe, it's the landing," he'd reply, as if the comedic response would bring her any relief.

With the sound of a running shower, Debbie knew she had a few minutes before Danny would be out. She tried not to remember, but it was no use.

****

"Daniel, where are you guys working today?" Debbie asked, as she put the finishing touches on her husband's lunch.

"Down in Aptos," replied Daniel, as he gulped down the last of his morning coffee.

"Please be careful," she asked. "You know how windy it can get there."

The 6' 4" muscular husband had no problem hoisting his 5' 100-pound wife up to his face.

"I'm part Mohawk Indian, remember? We don't fall," he said, with a grin from ear to ear.

"You're only 1/16th. That's hardly reassuring," she answered. But she put her arms around his neck and kissed him anyway, not only to comfort him, but to ease her own self-doubt.

****

The industrial park, located in Aptos California, spread over a 20-acre area bordering the cliffs. When the crew from Howard construction company arrived that morning, there was but a wisp of an on shore breeze coming off the ocean.

"Looks like the wind won't be much of an issue today," Bobby said to "Big Dan".

Dan looked skyward. The puffy cumulous clouds told a different story. The winds would come. He just hoped they'd be done and on the ground first.

Bobby Howard was the son of the boss of Howard construction. Unlike some sons, Bobby never took advantage of the fact his dad was the boss. He'd do any job he was asked, never expecting any favors. But the one thing Bobby Howard couldn't hide was his fear of heights. Ironic, the son of the boss of a construction company, afraid of heights. He hid it from everyone. Very few knew of the kid's anxiety, with the exception of Daniel Archer. Archer had been in some form of the construction business since he was 16. He had an innate sense of awareness when he sensed someone was uneasy.

The crane from US rentals arrived shortly after eight that morning. The job that day was fairly simple. The building they were working on was 100 feet long, 50 feet wide, with 60-foot-high walls and a metal roof. The roof supports had been delivered the previous day; 50-foot-long steel I-beams weighing nearly 1000 pounds each.

Two men on the ground would connect a steel cable to each end of a beam. In the middle of the cable was a steel connector which they would attach to the hook at the end of the crane's hoist cable. The crane operator's job was to slowly raise the beam to where it was waist high to the men on the wall's top plate. As the crane operator moved slowly to the back of the building, each worker, one on each wall, would walk with the beam to its appointed position. Using a bull pin, a ten-inch long piece of metal tapered at one end and inserted into a bolt hole at the end of the beam, they would guide the beam as well as maintain their balance. On a signal from one of the workers, the crane operator would slowly lower the beam onto the wall. Using their bull pins, the workers on the wall would align the holes of the beam to the holes on the wall plate and secure them with huge metal bolts and nuts. They were about halfway done when it was time for lunch break.

"How's it going up there today, Bobby?" Daniel asked.

"Like usual," Bobby sighed.

His shirt was soaked through with perspiration, a sign of just how much pressure the kid was under. Daniel felt for him.

"Look, I'll take your place after lunch. You've done enough already," said Daniel.

"Thanks anyway, Daniel. My dad expects me to be good at every aspect of the business. Walking the walls is one of them. I don't want to disappoint him or anyone else."

Daniel looked over to George, who had spent the morning walking one of the walls. He mouthed the words, 'you and me'. George nodded back that he understood. A boom truck took Daniel to the top of his wall, then George to the top of his wall.

"Keep an eye out guys, the wind's beginning to pick up," warned the boom truck operator.

Dan looked at George, who gave him a shoulder shrug, as if to suggest it might be best to call it a day. Dan smiled, waving off the caution of his friend, and gave him a thumbs up to take their position on the wall.

The front of the building was not quite due north, meaning the wind would be coming in at an angle to the dangling steel beams. George and Daniel had worked together for nearly 5 years. Rarely did they need to say anything to each other. They used hand signals to communicate.

They were about to set the last beam. There were about twelve feet between the last beam and the front of the roof. George and Daniel turned to face the wind as the boom operator began to raise the last beam. Daniel was using hand signals, telling the operator to keep raising the beam. When the beam was about waist high to them, Daniel signaled the boom operator to stop. He and George each grabbed their end of the beam and Daniel signaled the operator to slowly move the beam to the end of the roof.

The wind was really bothering George. Instead of placing his bull pin into the bolt hole, he held onto the beam with his hand. Daniel was more old school. He felt he had better control if he had his bull pin in the beam hole. They had only taken a few steps toward the end of the roof when a sudden gust of wind swept on the ocean. It was strong enough to cause the beam to sway toward them. George immediately let go of his grip and squatted to straddle the roof plate. Daniel had the same instinct, but before he could release his grip on his bull pin, the swaying beam pushed him backward at an awkward angle. He immediately released his grip, but it was too late. His balance point was gone. To those on the ground, it was like watching something in slow motion. Big Dan leaned to his right, his arms flailing in the air as if it would help him regain his balance. If he screamed, no one heard it. Between the wind blowing in off the ocean and the paralyzing fear that overcame them, they watched helplessly, as Big Dan's body fell to the ground.

****

Chapter 3

Dan and Debbie's home had been in the
Archer family for years. His mother and father deeded
it over to Debbie following Dan's death. There was no
way she could have afforded to live there on what she
made as an LVN at Dominican Hospital. She stared
again at the paper in her hand: a letter from Danny's
school counselor at Bay Elementary School. It
seemed despite his sub-average grades in the
classroom, her son scored in the 99th percentile on
every achievement test the school had given him. The
contrast between his test scores and classroom
performance was so drastic that Danny's guidance
counselor had made arrangements for the boy to take
the High School Aptitude Test at the end of the
seventh grade. The results came as no surprise to the
school counselor. Danny Archer placed in the 99th
percentile again.

****

The whistling of the teapot brought Debbie
Archer back to the present. She set the letter on the
table and went to make herself a cup of tea. With a
splash of milk and a bag of sweetener, Debbie stirred
her tea. Her mind drifted back to a conversation she

had had with Danny's school counselor following her husband's death.

"It's not unusual to see a student backslide academically when he's suffered the loss of one of his parents, as Danny has," Lois Brown, the counselor advised her. "It almost goes hand in hand in explaining his disciplinary problems."

Debbie shifted uneasily in her chair. She clutched a handkerchief in her right hand which she had already used more often than she wanted. In addition to poor academic performance, her son seemed to be in continuous trouble for fighting at school. Danny was big for his age. Sometimes he was challenged by older kids to see how tough he was. At other times, Danny wanted to show them how tough he was. He was also the one smaller kids ran to for protection from the school bullies.

"I know he's capable of doing much better," Debbie said. "I just don't know how to reach him. I don't want to put too much pressure on him, especially with his dad passing just five months ago."

"It's going to take time, Debbie," Lois said. "But he can make it. I know he can."

Lois had a pensive look on her face that troubled Debbie.

"What's bothering you?" she asked Lois.

Lois walked over to the door and closed it, then returned to her chair.

"Look, Debbie, I think we have a wonderful staff here at Bay and they do the very best they can, but there's only so much they can do when 30 plus students are competing for their attention. I think Danny would do better if you could get him into Holy Cross Catholic Elementary school. Their class size averages about 20 children and they have the money for extra classroom aides. And I think the discipline would help his impulse control."

Debbie slumped back in her chair.

"You might as well ask me to swim to Hawaii. I can't afford the tuition for a place like Holy Cross."

"I think if I write you a letter of recommendation and include Danny's test scores, Holy Cross may find some scholarship money to help. Besides, Father Duggan, the principal, is my brother. I'll see what I can do to speed the process," Lois said, as her face broke into a smile that told Debbie *it's in the bag*.

With a halfhearted sigh of relief that was meant more to reassure herself than the counselor, Debbie thanked Lois Brown and headed home. She dreaded the conversation she was going to have to have with Danny.

****

Newman surfed in the morning and then spent time working on the next chapter in his book. By 3:30 p.m. he was ready to leave. He folded up his chair, grabbed his board and was headed back to his truck when he saw Danny headed his way. He carried a small surfboard under one arm and his wetsuit in the other. *This can't be good*, Newman thought, *he hasn't even taken the time to put his wetsuit on.*

"Getting a late start aren't you?" Newman said to his young friend.

Danny said nothing. With more anger than a young boy his age should have, he jammed one leg and then the other into his wetsuit, then yanked up the top.

Newman unfolded his chair and sat down. "Okay my friend, we can play 20 questions or you can just tell me what's bothering you."

Danny turned to face him. Tears welled up in his eyes. He recounted to Newman the conversation he had had with his mother when she returned from her appointment with the school counselor. He wasn't working hard enough. He wasn't working up to his potential. He needed to do better.

"Now she's going to send me to that Catholic school, Holy Cross and I'm not even Catholic," he moaned. "They make you wear a uniform. I don't get it," he sighed. "I just want to surf."

Newman felt for the boy. Just wanting something doesn't make it happen. If it did, Newman's youth would have been much different.

"Take a look at those guys that are left out there," Newman said, pointing his finger to the last diehard dozen or so surfers still out in the water. "Recognize any of them?"

"Not from this far away. Besides, Newman, everyone's in their wetsuit."

"But if you were out there next to them, you'd recognize some of them, wouldn't you?" Newman queried the boy.

"Sure, I guess," Danny replied.

Newman put his arm over the boy's shoulders.

"Danny, your wetsuit is like your surfing uniform. Yes, you may look like anyone else from a distance, but up close and personal, everyone is different. There's a quote from Thomas Jefferson I want you to remember."

"Ok," Danny responded.

"In matters of taste, go with the flow. In matters of principle, stand as hard as a rock."

He might not get it right away, Newman thought. *But give him time at Holy Cross, and he would.*

Newman stood up and walked to the rail. "When you're out there and you decide to take the next wave, do you ever think, 'I'm not going to try as hard as I can to ride this wave out? How many days have you spent out on the water and decided to only try to surf the best you can on certain waves and not all waves?' "

"Never," the boy replied.

"So whether you ride the wave or it beats you, you still give every wave every bit of effort you've got, right?"

"Sure," pronounced the boy.

Danny headed down the stairs to the shore. Part way down, he looked back at Newman and smiled. Newman smiled back and decided to stay a little longer. He was there about an hour later when Danny got out of the water. He set his board down next to Newman's chair and took off his wetsuit.

"Any idea why they're still out there?" Newman asking, gesturing to the last few die hard surfers still out there.

"Because they wanted to do what I wanted to do, surf."

"Actually it's more than wanting to just surf, Danny. They want to get better. They're not out there just to be average."

"Ok...?" Danny responded with a look of bewilderment on his face.

"Why would you want to be average at anything?" Newman said.

"I only care about surfing," the defiant adolescent answered.

"Yes, of course. How could I have forgotten," Newman said. "I was just wondering if you thought of school as being in a surfing class, would you really settle for being average? Wouldn't you want to be the best surfer you could possibly be?"

Newman folded his chair, put his note pad under his arm and was about to head home when two surfers hit the top of the stairs.

"You still hanging out here, Newman?" asked the taller of the two.

"No place else I'd rather be," Newman replied. "Besides, I still have work to do, and speaking of work, are you still with the Santa Cruz PD?"

The tall one, Bill, smiled. "No place else I'd rather be," he chuckled.

"And you Freddy, still working at Burke Preparatory?"

"It's not work when you love what you're doing, Newman. You taught me that," Fred answered. "And the answer is yes. You're looking at the Dean of Student Affairs and on top of that, they straddled me with being the chairman of the Faculty/Student Committee."

"Guys," Newman said. "Meet my friend, Danny Archer. Danny, this is Bill Evans and Fred Wyckoff, old friends of mine."

The three shook hands.

"Newman giving you surf lessons, Danny?" Bill asked.

"When the time's right, he does," Danny answered.

Both Bill and Fred started to laugh. "Not that old line. Damn Newman, you need to get some new material," Fred said.

The look of wonderment on Danny's face demanded an explanation.

"Kid, when we were about your age, maybe a little older, we begged Newman to teach us to surf. That's all we wanted to do. He'd always say, 'when the time's right,' and when we asked, 'when will the time be right? he'd say, 'when all your work at home is done.'"

The two men headed off toward the market when Fred suddenly turned around.

"Listen to what Newman tells you, Danny. It's more than just surfing he's talking about."

Danny wasn't completely processing what Fred meant, but his wheels were turning. The smile grew on Newman's face

****

Chapter 4

It was late in the afternoon when Debbie finally found a parking spot near Holy Cross Church. The huge white cathedral-like structure was surrounded by a four-foot high granite wall. A large arch served as an entryway to the steps leading up to the church doors. There was nothing resembling a school, much less offices, that Debbie could see. Between her frustration with her son's behavior and the apprehension of meeting the school principal, Debbie didn't notice the stranger who had parked on the opposite side of the street from them. She and Danny had a 4 p.m. appointment with the principal. She got out of the car and walked around to the passenger side.

"Well, are you going to sit there or are you going to get out?"

He slammed his head against the head rest. After a few moments, his hand jerked the door handle up and he got out, slamming the door shut. The boy defiantly shoved his hands into his pants pockets. Debbie was glancing down at a piece of paper in her hand, looking completely lost when the stranger walked up to them.

"Need directions?" he asked, setting his surfboard down.

Debbie raised her head, feeling relieved at the offer of assistance. When she noticed his long brown hair braided into a pony tail, a faded looking swim suit and a surf board under his arm, the last thing she felt was relief.

"Thanks," she replied. "We've got an appointment with the principal of Holy Cross. Do you have any idea where the school office is located?"

Picking up his surf board, the man said, "Follow me."

They walked a half a block to the corner, made a left, then walked another short block.

"That's the school parking lot across the street. Walk through it and you'll see two long buildings with a lawn between them. The one on the right is the classrooms and the one on the left is the administration offices. The first door is the secretary's office. They can probably help you there," he said.

"Thank you," Debbie said.

"No problem," answered the stranger, as he headed on his way.

"Let's go," Debbie said to Danny, who was leaning against the car, arms folded tightly across his chest as if to say, *Make me!*

This isn't going to be easy, Debbie thought. "Danny, I said let's go." The firmness in her voice barely caused the boy to look up.

"Why?" he snapped.

"We've been over this a hundred times. Your counselor at Bay thinks the smaller classes at Holy Cross will help you. Now, no more stalling. You've got to give this a try."

With insolent resignation, Danny walked with his mother to the office the stranger had pointed out to them.

****

"May I help you?" asked Mary Woodson, the school secretary.

"Yes, my name is Debbie Archer. This is my son, Danny. We have an appointment with Father Duggan."

"Father Duggan isn't here right now. Sister Agnes, the Vice-Principal, is handling his appointments today. I'll page her."

Moments later, Sister Agnes appeared. Her demeanor would have petrified the staunchest of Catholics, let alone non-Catholics like the Archers. She appeared to be slightly over five feet tall. Her rotund figure made her look like an emperor penguin what with her black robes and white starched collar. She adjusted an oversized rosary which hung around her waist like a belt. Her right hand hung next to a large crucifix dangling at the end of the rosary. Her fingers twitched slightly as if she were a gunslinger in the old west about to draw down on the sheriff. But it was her face that practically caused both Danny and his mother to gasp. Crows' feet wrinkles spread out from the corner of her piercing brown eyes. A small scar arched across her right cheek. Her face in general looked bleached. No doubt corporal punishment was no stranger to this one. *What am I getting Danny into?* Debbie thought.

"How may I help you?" the stentorian tone to her voice caused both Debbie and Danny to flinch. Danny instinctively stepped backward. When they didn't answer right away, the nun's fingers grasped the dangling rosary as if she was going to swing it at them. There was a martinet glare in her eyes.

"I have an appointment with a Father Duggan about getting my son, Danny, into Holy Cross," Debbie said.

"I'm handling his appointments today," the nun answered. "Come with me."

Debbie and Danny followed the nun down the hallway to the last office on the left. The dark hallway was alight with enough small candles you could practically feel the heat. The walls were cluttered with so many pictures of Jesus through various stages of his life, one might think his office was at the end of the hallway. The sign over the door read, "Vice-Principal/Dean of Discipline." Sister Agnes opened the door, then pointed for them to go in. Debbie felt as if the warden was directing her into the gas chamber.

"So, you want to come to Holy Cross?" she asked.

"Yes, that's why we're here," Debbie answered.

"I was asking the boy," came the terse reply from the Vice-Principal.

With a panicked look in his eyes, Danny looked at his mother. Debbie nodded at him to answer.

"I guess so," he murmured.

"I guess so isn't good enough, young man," the nun snapped back. "Either you want to or you don't, which is it?"

Debbie's sense of intimidation quickly faded. *You bitch!* She thought. Like a lioness protecting her cub, Debbie leaned forward in her chair.

"Sister Agnes, I want what's best for my son. Danny is not Catholic, so it's a little unfair to asked him if he wants to be here, if religion is the point of your question. The point is if Holy Cross is as good as it is portrayed educationally, then I want him here and that should be good enough. Your job is to make him want to be here."

Sister Agnes was not used to being questioned.

"Perhaps you should look at these," Debbie said, handing Sister Agnes the letter from Lois Brown, Danny's counselor, as well as his latest test scores.

Sister Agnes perused the documents.

"I see more potential than results," she said, placing the papers on her desk.

"Well, isn't that what every parent brings you, a child with potential?" Debbie said, leaning back in her chair. *Take that*, she thought.
"I see you will be needing financial support," Sister Agnes said. "What are you and your husband able to pay?"

"My husband is dead," Debbie responded. "I work as an LVN at Dominican Hospital. Perhaps I can volunteer here at the school as a health aid?"

"Mrs. Archer, your request for financial aid will have to be reviewed by our admissions committee. As I'm sure you are aware, there are many needy Catholic families trying to get their children into Holy Cross."

Why not reject it now, Debbie thought.

The phone on Sister Agnes' desk rang.

"Yes, I'm with someone," she snapped. Within seconds, she said, "I'll send them in." Turning her attention to Debbie, Sister Agnes said, "Father Duggan's here now. He'll see you in his office. Come with me."

Sister Agnes took them across the hallway. She knocked on the door. From within a voice said, "Come in."

Sister Agnes opened the door and said, "Mrs. Archer and her son, Danny, are here to see you about admission to Holy Cross."

"Thank you," the voice said.

"Father Duggan will see you," Sister Agnes said, as if they were getting an audience with the Queen of England.

If Debbie Archer and her son were shocked when they saw Sister Agnes, that doesn't describe their reaction when they saw Father Duggan and his office. He was the stranger who had given them directions to the school office. The walls of his office were adorned with autographed pictures of famous sports celebrities from the Bay Area; Willie Mays, Willie McCovey, Bobby Bonds, Joe Perry, John Brodie, you name them. Debbie's late husband was a huge sports fan. She recognized all of them.

****

The shocked look on their faces caused the priest to chuckle.

"You probably expected the more traditional black pants, black shirt and white collar," he said, arranging a couple of chairs for Debbie and Danny. "I had a chance to get a couple of hours off which doesn't happen often, so I took advantage of it to do a little surfing. Please have a seat."

"I wasn't sure what to expect. We're not Catholic, but the surfing did catch me off guard," Debbie replied. Danny sat in his chair, speechless.

"So my big sister sent you, did she?" grinned the priest, as he glanced over the papers Sister Agnes had given him.

"Well, she seems to think the small class size and extra attention will help Danny," Debbie said.

"From these percentile results, I'd say Danny doesn't need much help," the priest responded.

"But his grades don't come anywhere near what he's capable of," Debbie answered.

The priest adjusted his pony tail. "You know, since these are Danny's grades, let's ask him what he thinks."

If he could have melted into the wall, he would have, but there was no place for Danny to hide. The priest set the papers on a table next to his chair. He stretched out his legs, clasped his hands behind his head and asked, "Danny, what do you think the best possible grades are?"

Danny looked at his mother, his eyes pleading for her to answer for him.

"Go ahead, Danny, answer Father Duggan."

"I don't like to stand on formality, Mrs. Archer, so why not call me Father Mike."

Danny turned his head toward the priest. "I guess all A's." The timidity in the boy's tone caused his voice to crack. A nudge from his mother caused Danny to quickly add, "Father Mike."

"Maybe I can take a little of the pressure off you, Danny. I don't care if you get all A's, all B's or all C's. Those letters are not the least bit important to me," the priest said.

The only person more surprised at hearing the priest's words than Danny was his mother.

"Father Mike, it's important to me that Danny gets good grades so that maybe he'll have a chance to go to college and have a successful life," Debbie said. The look on her face could not have been more obvious, *Why am I explaining this to you?*

"Why don't we asked Danny? Tell me what's in your heart, son. Is getting good grades important to you?" the priest asked.

This time there was no turning to his mother. Something about Father Mike made Danny feel at ease, like he could really be honest.

"Not really," the boy answered. Then he added, "I'm sorry, Mom, but he said to say what was in my heart."

Maybe this was all for naught. Maybe he doesn't belong at Holy Cross after all, especially if the principal feels the way he does, Debbie thought.

Father Mike sat upright in his chair. "Danny, let me tell you what's important to me and what's really important to your mother." The priest slid his chair so close to Danny's chair that their knees touched. "Whenever I ask you, how are things going, I expect to hear, I'm trying my best, Father. If you can do that, your mother will be happy. I'll be happy, and your teachers at Holy Cross will be happy. The letter grades will take care of themselves. Trust me."

It wasn't like Danny Archer could simply put his trust in Father Mike. After all, he was a perfect stranger, and a priest at that, which only increased Danny's apprehension. However, there was something engaging about the way Father Mike talked to him, like he was really concerned about how Danny felt and what was important to him. Newman's words at their last meeting began to play in his mind. *Did you ever not try your best on every wave?"*

Father Mike moved his chair back and walked to his desk. He picked up a small packet of papers.

"This is an application for financial aid. I'll need it by the end of next week, assuming you still want to come to Holy Cross."

"I think we do, don't we, Danny?"

A smile from the priest brought a shoulder shrug from the boy.

Chapter 5

The two boys sat on their surf boards. Several sets of waves had come and gone with neither boy making an effort to catch one.

"I don't get it, Danny. I thought we would graduate from Bay together," Fletcher Williams said to his best friend. "Now, you're going to Holy Cross! Who's going to be my best friend?"

How could Danny explain to his friend what he didn't really understand himself?

"Gee, Fletch, it's not like I'm going to the North Pole. You're still gonna be my best friend and we're still gonna surf together. Besides, this guy, Father Mike, he surfs. How cool is that!"

Fletcher glanced over his shoulder at the next wave, then turned to Danny.

"I need to take this one alone."

Watching his friend ride off on the wave only added to the angst that had consumed Danny since they'd received the acceptance letter to Holy Cross a week ago. At first it was cool that Father Mike surfed and yes, Newman's words of advice had given Danny a short-lived sense of confidence. But they weren't going to a new school where they didn't know anyone. They weren't the ones leaving their friends behind. And his teachers at Bay—he didn't really like them, but at least he knew what to expect from them. Suddenly, he felt all alone, and going to Holy Cross didn't seem like such a good idea after all. Damn, he wished his father were here.

****

The summer before Danny was to start the eighth grade at Holy Cross was worse than anything Debbie Archer could have imagined. Danny sunk to an all-time low. Every request to help out around the house was met with "Why?" Every threat of consequence was met with "I don't care." Debbie might as well have had her meals in solitary confinement in a maximum security prison for all the conversation she got from her son. Danny had been spending less time with his friend, Fletcher, and more time with some kids Debbie knew had bad reputations. Debbie had shared her frustration with Tara, one of the two women who lived in the studio cottage behind her house. Tara was a supervisor with the Santa Cruz Recreation Department. The shared backyard deck became a place where Debbie could bare her soul to Tara.

"Some more?" Debbie asked, holding out a freshly opened bottle of chardonnay.

"Only if you have more hummus and crackers," answered Tara.

"On the way," replied Debbie, as she headed through the back door into the kitchen.

When she returned, Debbie sank into her Adirondack chair.

"I've tried everything, Tara. Nothing works," she moaned. "No reward is good enough, no consequence is bad enough. I work days. I can't chain him to the house. If I change my schedule to nights, then who's going to watch him?"

Tara and her partner, Becka, had lived in the small cottage behind Debbie's house for years. They loved Daniel and Debbie and had come to think of Danny as their own child.

"You know, Debbie, the Rec Department has plenty of summer programs for kids Danny's age. Maybe I could get him into one of the programs I run."

"I don't know, Tara. In some ways, Danny is wise beyond his years. He'd probably figure out it's just a way for you to keep an eye on him for me."

"If I can't out maneuver a twelve-year old, it's time for me to get out of the recreation business. Let's see, ok?"

****

It had not been a good day for Danny Archer, but then what day had been of late? Besides going to a new school for the eighth grade, his friend, Fletcher, was on a two-week vacation with his family. Though they had drifted apart recently, Danny still missed him. Danny needed to talk to Newman. His mom would be home soon and his chores were still not done. He didn't care. He needed to talk to Newman. Danny changed into his wetsuit, grabbed his board and headed to the ocean, a block and a half away. As he approached East Cliff Drive, a sense of relief come over him. He saw Newman sitting in his chair.

"Hi Newman," Danny said, setting his board down next to Newman's chair.

"What's up kid? Ready for a lesson?"

Any other time, Danny's answer would have been a simple yes and he'd head down the stairs to the beach. Today though, he needed to talk.

"Can I ask you a question, Newman?"

Newman shut his notebook and put it in his bag. "Ask away," he said.

For the next hour, Danny Archer poured out his soul to Newman. It was an emotional roller coaster. Danny knew he hadn't tried his best at school, but he promised his mother he'd do much better if she would let him stay at Bay. He was leaving his best friend, Fletcher, behind to go to a school where he didn't know a soul. He was going to have to take a city bus to and from school and that meant less time during the week to surf. With each emotional plea, Danny's voice cracked and tears welled up in his eyes.

"Newman, it's just not fair!"

If you think this isn't fair, wait till you see what life has in store for you, Newman thought. The boy didn't need that bucket of ice water thrown on him right now. Newman knew what he needed.

"Put your board in the back of my truck," Newman said. "We're going somewhere."

"My mom's due home anytime now," Danny said.

"I'll handle your mother. You get in the truck."

Newman and the boy headed up 36th avenue to Danny's house. Debbie's car was in the driveway. Newman went up to the front door while Danny waited in the truck.
He watched his mom and Newman talk. Debbie looked around Newman and blew her son a kiss.

"Have fun!" she hollered.

Newman got back into his truck and they headed up 36th avenue to Portola, then turned left toward Santa Cruz. Danny sat silent, until they pulled into the parking lot near the Dream Inn.

"What are we doing here," he asked.

"We're going to Cowells beach," Newman answered.

"Gee, Newman, I've never surfed here before. Do you think I'm good enough?" Danny asked with about as much confidence as Wilbur Wright had when he said to his brother that historic day, "Do you really think this thing can fly?"

"Only one way to find out, Danny. Now let's go."

Danny picked up his board to follow Newman when he noticed Newman wasn't carrying his board.

"Hey Newman, where's your board?"

"I'm not surfing. You are."

"But you said we were going to surf Cowells," Danny pleaded.

"No, I said we were going to Cowells."

Newman knelt down on the sand and stared at the ocean.

"Know who made surfing famous in Santa Cruz, Danny?"

"You," Danny said, sounding both sarcastic and naive at the same time.

"Very funny," Newman chuckled. "No, actually it was three Hawaiian princes who came here in 1885 and put on a surfing demonstration where the San Lorenzo River hits the ocean. They used long boards made of redwood. It was quite the show."

Newman stood up, brushing the sand from his knees. "There's a lot to learn from surfing, Danny."

Just then, a couple on a tandem bicycle rode past them, and headed down the pier.

"You see that?" Newman said, pointing to the couple.

"Sure," answered Danny, more confused than ever.

"Ever see two people on a tandem surf board? He asked.

"No."

"Danny, you and Fletcher are not going to ride through life on a tandem surf board, and you're not going to spend the rest of your life surfing Pleasure Point. There are places to surf all over this planet that you've never heard of—exotic and dangerous places where only the best surfers in the world go. If you ever get a chance to surf one of those places, will you go or will you stay safe and surf Pleasure Point? Everything connected with going to Holy Cross is no different. Now, head out to the peak. I'll watch from here."

****

Chapter 6

Danny's love of surfing was not shared by his two new acquaintances, Joey Alders and Sammy Baker. They were a year ahead of Danny at Bay Elementary and predicted by the staff to wind up in Juvenile Hall before they finished high school. Danny had already been involved in a couple of scraps with the two against other kids at the Boardwalk. Danny was sitting on the front porch when Butch and Eddy rode up on their bicycles.

"Hey, Danny, get your bike and meet us at the Seven-Eleven. We're gonna score some beer," Joey said, as he nervously tried to light a cigarette.

The little voice inside Danny's head practically screamed, "Don't go, stupid." But Danny was nearly thirteen, and stupid is what kids do at that age.

"Give me a minute," Danny said, as he headed inside his house.

'Please do your breakfast dishes' was his mother's last request before she headed to work. He stacked them in the sink—close enough to washing for him. He hustled out the back door, got on his bike and headed up 36th avenue and down Portola Drive to the Seven-Eleven. When the three arrived at the Seven-Eleven, Joey revealed his plan.

"The old gook who owns this dump always has a stack of beer that's going on sale just inside the door. I'll walk in, look around for a second or two, then jam a couple of six packs in my backpack and out the door. Easy as can be!" gloated Joey.

Sammy laughed, "Cool. Let's do it."

Again the little voice screamed, *Don't do this, stupid!* Once again, Danny didn't listen.

"You in?" Sammy asked.

"Heck yes," came his response.

****

"You like motors, Bill?" asked Hal Wilson, his former partner.

"I like the open air instead of a patrol car," Evans answered, patting his Harley-Davidson, which the Santa Cruz PD recently adopted for its motorcycle division.

"I get all the fresh air I need with the window down," chuckled Wilson from inside his patrol car, "and I stay a hell of a lot dryer when it rains."

To each his own, Evans thought, as he scanned up and down Portola Drive. Two kids on bicycles would not normally get Evan's attention. Three kids on bicycles leaning against the side wall of a liquor store at 8:30 in the morning was another matter. *Could be nothing*, Evans thought. After all it was summer time. But then maybe not. The first hint of trouble was when the boy wearing a backpack handed his bike to the other two and headed into the liquor store. The remaining two moved their bicycles to the sidewalk headed down the avenue to the ocean. Now 30th avenue was a one-way street pointed to Portola Drive and that would soon prove problematic for Evans and his former partner. The boy who had gone into the liquor store suddenly came running out the door. His backpack was practically dragging on the ground. He met his waiting friends and they headed down 30th avenue, pedaling as fast as they could. The store owner, an elderly Vietnamese man named Dinh, stood in the street screaming at them.

"See that?" asked Evans.

"Yep," answered Wilson, turning on the ignition to his patrol car. "I'll head down 32nd. You take 34th."

"Got it," answered Evans, who had flipped up his kick stand and reved up his Harley.

Thieves are generally not smart people and adolescent thieves take smart to its lowest level. Evans and Wilson drove slowly, checking visually with each other at intersecting streets. When they got to Flora, they saw what they were looking for. Half way down the block, three bicycles were leaning against a garage door. Evans recognized the yellow one as the one the kid with the backpack was riding. They approached the garage from opposite directions.

"Do you smell what I do?" Evans whispered to Wilson.

"I believe I do," answered Wilson with a smile, the undeniable aroma of marijuana.

Evans quickly made a visual check around each corner of the garage.

"Side door on the right," he said. "Gimme a ten count, then pound on the door."

Wilson nodded affirmative. Evans worked his way down the side of the garage to the door. When he heard Wilson yell, "Police, open up," he raised his right foot, a size 15 motorcycle boot, about six inches of the ground. The first out the door was the kid with the backpack. He did a complete summersault with the remaining beer cans tumbling out of his backpack onto the ground. The next two quickly followed and between trying to avoid their fallen friend and the beer cans they soon found themselves sprawled out on the ground.

"My, my, my, what do we have here?" Evans asked.

****

Mary Salazar of the Juvenile Probation Department finished reading the reports.

"Joey Alders and Sammy Baker are frequent fliers with Probation, everything from snatch and grabs to vandalism up and down Portola Drive. This isn't the first time they've hit the Seven-Eleven so they'll be spending the next few weeks in Juvenile Hall until the Court figures out what to do with them. This kid, Archer, never heard of him," she said.

"Do you mind if I talk with him, Mary?" Evans asked.

"Be my guest. He's in the cage at the end of the hall."

From the moment he was placed in the police car, Danny felt panic like never before in his life. Alders and Baker sat stoic next to him. Neither said a word. For Danny, there was no gangster wannabe bravado. He was scared, really scared. He sat on the bench, his arms wrapped around his drawn up knees. Evans opened the door to the holding cage, a 10X10 room with benches around three walls.

"Danny Archer?" he asked.

"Yes sir," came the whispered response.

"Come with me," Evans said. As they passed the men's room, Evans asked, "Do you need to use this?"

With the nodding of the kid's head, Evans pushed the door open. It was a good thing because another second and there would have been a hazmat spill in the hall way. Evans heard the flush of the urinal, running water in the sink, then the kid appeared. Once inside the interview room, Evans sat next to Danny, instead of at his customary spot on the other side of the table.

"Where do you live, Danny?"

"529 36th Avenue, sir."

"I know that area. You surf much?"

"Yes sir."

Evans looked closely at the boy. Unlike the other two boys whose eyes had radiated defiance, this kid was really afraid. Evans guessed he could play Father Flannigan, not Joe Friday. He was right.

"How do you think your parents are going to feel when they find out about this?"

Danny's hands trembled as he wiped the tears now running down his face. His head hung as he mumbled, "My dad is dead, sir, and my mom, well she's going to be really mad."

Bill Evans knew how to apply the law, but to the chagrin of his supervisor, he also knew how to apply the spirit of the law. This was a time for the latter, not the former.

"I think first she's going to be scared and disappointed, then she'll be mad. Mad as hell!"

Danny looked up at Evans. "Yes sir, she will."

Evans let his arm rest on the boy's shoulders. "Maybe it's time I take you home, what do you say?"

All Danny could do was nod his head.

****

Really! All I asked you to do was do the breakfast dishes, Debbie thought, as she looked at the pile of unwashed dishes in the sink. She let out a sigh and hung her head. *Could things possibly get any worse?* With the knock on the front door, she was about to find out. She opened the front door to see a police officer and her son standing there.

"I'm Officer Evans, Mrs. Archer. May I come in?"

"Oh my God! What's happened?" she gasped. "Danny, are you alright?"

The boy flew into his mother's open arms. "I'm sorry Mom, I'm really sorry," he mumbled.

Debbie motioned for the officer to come in. It didn't take long for Evans to explain what had happened and what he thought Danny's role had amounted to.

"It was Joey Alders who actually stole the beer from the Seven-Eleven and it was Alders who was in possession of the marijuana," Evans concluded.

"But Danny was still there. He was with them," Debbie asked, her arms now holding her son as if to protect him from the consequences.

"Yes he was, Mrs. Archer," Evan answered. "Danny will have to meet with a Probation officer who will make a recommendation to the Judge in Juvenile

Court. But he's never been in any trouble before so I don't think it's going to be too bad."

"Sweetheart, I need to talk with Officer Evans."

Danny understood. He gave his mother a hug, then left for his room.

"Will he have any kind of a criminal record?" Debbie asked. "Danny's been accepted into Holy Cross and something like this could cause them to reject him before he even starts."

"Criminal record, no," Evans said. "But there will be a record of his case and adjudication with the Probation Department. As far as Holy Cross is concerned, I know the principal, Father Mike. I'll have a talk with him."

"How do you know him?" Debbie asked.

"Oh, years ago, Mike, myself and another friend, Fred, learned to surf right down the street at Pleasure Point."

"Gosh, there is a man who has kind of befriended Danny and gives him surfing lessons there. Perhaps you know him? His name is Newman."

Evans started laughing. "Are you kidding me?" he said. "Newman taught all three of us how to surf. If Newman's looking after Danny, he's going to be ok. Believe me."

****

It wasn't like her son had made a 180 over the last few days. Yes, there was less arguing and sometimes his chores were done when she asked. Besides worrying about the Probation Department, there was still a sense of resignation about going to Holy Cross.

"Can I come in?" Tara asked, as she opened the door to the kitchen.

"Please do," Debbie said. "I'll put the tea pot on."

Debbie used a bit of agave to sweeten her tea. "So what's up?" she asked.

"Remember that job at the Rec Department we talked about?" Tara said. "Well, I talked with my boss about it. What with budget cuts and loss of I don't know how many positions, he'll support anything that will keep programs afloat. So here's the deal. Danny will work with me. I need help with the swimming program. I may be able to swing a small stipend and he'll get credit from taking care of equipment, cleaning up the locker room and shower areas. His name will appear on the staff chart for the summer. What do you think? "

"I think with what happened last week, this is just what he needs," Debbie said. She filled Tara in on the details.

"Well, now's as good as time as any to talk with him," Tara said. "Danny, it's me, Tara. Can I talk with you for a minute?"

Danny came out of his bedroom, barely awake. He shuffled to the sink for a drink of water.

"Why so early, Tara?"

Tara smiled. Now she'd get a chance to work her magic.

"I've got to go to work and I needed to talk with you about something before I go," she said, taking a sip of tea.

"Sure, Tara. What's up?" he replied, taking a seat at the table.

"I've got to get ready for work. You two talk," Debbie said, heading off to her bedroom.

"Look, Danny. I run a program at the Rec Department teaching swimming lessons to small kids. My bosses want to stop the program."

"Why would they want to do that?" Danny asked.

"Same old thing we hear every year, Danny. Not enough money to hire the people we need. I lost my student assistant at the beginning of the summer and I can't keep up with the workload. I need help. That's where you come in."

Danny Archer was no lazy twelve-year old. He worked around the neighborhood getting what Debbie called charity jobs to earn extra money. But this was different.

"Are you interested?" Tara asked.

"I guess so," Danny said. *I guess so* is adolescent code for I need to know more.

"Danny, this isn't some charity job. I really need the help and you'll get paid."

That got his attention. He pushed aside the bowl of cereal his mom had ready for him when he sat down at the table.

"What would I do?" he asked.

Good, she thought. *What would I do, not how much will I get paid.*

"You'll be responsible for keeping a count of how many float boards we have and handing them out to each swimmer, make sure the pool side is clear of towels and chairs left by other swimmers, clean up the shower and locker rooms after each class. I give four one hour lessons with a half hour break between each lesson. I have enough money in my budget to pay you $4.25 an hour. Now, this doesn't sound like much; however, I'm going to list you on the swimming program guide as my summer intern. No extra pay for it, but sometimes it looks good on your record."

Danny Archer was a smart kid, but he was a twelve-year old smart and he had no idea how much this swimming gig would benefit him.

"I'll have to talk with Mom," Danny said. Now his voice had a sense of eagerness in it.

"Oh, absolutely," Tara said, knowing she had landed her fish.

Fortunately, Debbie Archer had already been briefed by Tara, because if she had to make sense out of her son's rambling, fractured sentences, her son was going to be a swimming instructor with his own class and in charge of maintenance and equipment.

"Honey, that's so exciting. I know you'll do a great job for Tara," Debbie said, trying to calm down her overly excited son to a point where his heart beat was under 130.

****

Chapter 7

"Are you ready?" she asked.

Danny adjusted his orange vest with 'staff' stenciled on the back, and put the lanyard with his id card over his head. With more apprehension than confidence, he said, "Yes."

"Don't worry, Danny. The first day is the hardest," Tara said.

She had explained to Danny how the program would work. There would be about 25 eight-year olds in the class. Every one of them had completed the water safety and beginner swimming class. The pool was fifty feet long, twenty-five feet wide and four feet deep. A line of red floats was strung from side to side and about twenty feet from the end of the pool She would have kids in groups of four swim from the end of the pool to the float line and back. Danny was to stay with the other kids until it was their turn. Tara needed this extra set of eyes. Yes, the kids would be instructed to keep one hand on the side of the pool, but the temptation to push away on their styrofoam boards was often too great. The last half hour was free play.

"I'll be in the water with you. It's really important for you to keep your eyes moving at all times, ok?"

"You bet," Danny said, as he slid into the pool.

****

After the first week, Danny had almost forgotten about his pending hearing with the Probation agent, Mary Salazar. Tara had praised Danny for his attention to the kids. Not once had Tara had to remind him to do something. At the Rec pool, his spirits seemed up. Still hanging over his head though, was the pending meeting with the Probation Officer and having to go to Holy Cross. At least, there was Newman.

****

He smiled to himself as he read the last paragraph. *Not bad if I do say so*, he thought, setting his pen down and closing his notebook.

"Newman, have you been out today?" Danny asked, already in his wet suit and with surf board in hand.

"Yep, once this morning and ready to go again," he answered.

The two headed down the stairs to the beach. Newman adjusted his wet suit while Danny straightened out his leash line.

"So how's the new job working out?" Newman asked.

"Not bad," Danny answered. "I'm in the water and Tara's really cool."

Newman smiled. "What do you plan to do with all the money you're making?"

"Actually, I was thinking about getting a new surf board," Danny said, as he attached his leash line to his ankle.

"So you're sacrificing your time to work so you can better enjoy surfing, are you?"

Danny looked at him. "Newman, I'm just buying a new surf board. What's the mystery there?"

He's only twelve, Newman told himself. *Don't expect too much too soon.*

When they got through the last breaking wave, they turned their boards at an angle toward the shore. It helped them keep an eye out for the next set of waves. They didn't do much talking for the next hour or so. They took as many waves as they could, sometimes together, sometimes separately. It pleased Newman to see the progress Danny was making. *He really has a natural talent*, Newman thought.

"Nice ride," Newman said to Danny when he returned from his last wave.

"Thanks," Danny replied.

Suddenly Newman jumped to his knees, his hands held above his eye brows to help sharpen his focus.

"What is it?" Danny asked.

"There," Newman hollered, pointing to a lone surf board rolling onto the sand.

He stared to his left, then to his right. When he finally saw a surfer struggling to his feet and heading toward the beached surf board, he sat down.

"I hate to see a lone board. It can be a sign of real trouble," he said.

Danny glanced back toward the sun. He'd better get home. His mom would be there soon.

"I got to go, Newman," Danny said.

"Let me guess, your mom's getting home soon and there were chores not done."

The impish grin told Newman the kid was still a work in progress.

"Tell me about the job," Newman asked.

Paddling into shore, Danny brought Newman up to speed.

"I like working with the kids more than I thought," Danny said.

"And how's that mess with the Probation Department working out?"

Danny looked at Newman with a *how did you know about that* look in his eyes.

"Do I really need to explain how I know? Just tell me what's happening."

"I go for my hearing next Friday. Officer Evans told my mom he didn't think anything too serious was going to happen."

"Well, Bill's a pretty good judge when it comes to this type of thing. I'd trust him if I were you."

Now Danny was really surprised. "How do you know Officer Evans?" he asked.

"Who do you think taught him how to surf?" Newman replied, while stifling his laughter.

"Remember the first time you took a wave and realized too late it was bigger than you thought?" Newman said, as they waded ashore.

"Man, that was a big mistake," Danny sighed.

"How about the time you rode that wave too far toward the rocks and I had to pull you out?"

"Yeah, another mistake on my part," Danny answered as he finished getting out of his wet suit.

Newman laid his wet suit over his chair. "Sometimes you need to listen to that little voice inside your head. You know, the one that says, 'wave's too big' or 'curl out now' or whatever. Making mistakes is unavoidable. You choose whether to learn from them."

"I just hope someday I'll quit making mistakes out there." Danny answered.

"Son, that's not going to happen. We go out day after day to be better than we were the day before."

"See ya later, Newman," Danny said, as he headed home.

Newman watched the kid cross East Cliff Drive and head up 36th avenue. *I plant the seed. It's all I can do. I just plant the seed.*

****

His week went like clockwork, as far as Tara was concerned. Danny was really attentive to those kids waiting for their turn with Tara. It was during free play where he really shined. Tara noticed he seemed to be everywhere, weaving between splashing kids whose outside voices often reached double digit decibels. The second week started out the same. By Thursday of the second week, Tara had quit keeping her third eye out on Danny. They were getting ready for the last class of the day. Danny counted off each swimmer and gave them their float board.

"Full class, Tara," Danny called out.

"Ok everyone. Let's get our faces wet." On her command, everyone put their faces underwater.

"Now, will the first five swimmers come over to me."

Five minnow-like swimmers pushed away from the end of the pool and, using their float board, kicked their way to Tara. When she was done instructing them, they kicked their way back to the end of the pool and the next five came out. Finally, Tara was done.

"Ok, everyone. You've got free play for half an hour," Tara shouted to her class.

Danny liked to watch the kids from the center of the play area so he waded out to his spot. Tara headed to the right side of the pool to talk with a couple of parents. That's when it happened. One of the things Newman had drilled into him was, if you ever see a surf board without a rider, keep your eyes on the lookout. The yelling and hollering of the kids was suddenly drowned out when Tara heard Danny scream, "Tara, Tara!"

Tara turned in time to see Danny dive beneath the single styrofoam board floating in the center of the play area. She hadn't taken two steps when Danny surfaced, holding an eight-year girl with eyes as big as saucer plates. She was coughing up water. She was too scared to cry, trying to get her breath between spitting out water. Once she got her breath, the crying came. Tara finally had the child calmed down when her mother arrived.

"She swallowed a little water, that's all, thanks to Danny," Tara told the mother, who was now anxiously rocking her daughter back and forth.

"Sweetie, what happened?" her mother asked.

"I thought I could swim without my board. I should have listened to Danny. He said never let go of your board. I'm sorry, Mommy."

The mother cupped her hand behind her daughter's head and held her tight against her breasts.

"It's ok, Vanessa," she said. "Next time you remember what Danny tells you, ok?"

The girl hugged her mother even tighter while nodding her head yes. When the mother was finished thanking Danny, she turned to Tara. "Are you sure there's nothing I can do for that young man?"

"You know, there is," Tara said.

She explained how a letter of appreciation would do wonders for a situation Danny was involved in.

"You'll have it in the morning," the mother said.

When the mother was gone, Tara sat down. Now it was her nerves that needed calming down. She closed her eyes and took a deep breath. When she opened her eyes, Danny was sitting next to her.

"I'm sorry, Tara. I really was trying to keep my eyes on everyone," Danny said. "When I saw that board floating, I knew something was wrong."

"You did just fine, Danny," she said, putting her arm around his shoulder. "You saw something was wrong and you acted immediately. I think you're the hero today."

Word of what happened at the pool spread like wildfire through the Rec Department and beyond. That afternoon, a reporter from the Santa Cruz Sentinel was knocking on Debbie Archer's front door. The reporter took a picture of Danny and talked with him about saving the little girl.

****

Chapter 8

The silence was deafening inside the car as Debbie Archer drove her son to his meeting with the Probation Officer. When they had parked and gotten out of the car, a familiar face greeted them. It was Officer Bill Evans.

"Thought you could use a little moral support," he said. "Mary's holding the meeting in her office since the judge has already signed off on her recommendation."

"Do you know what it is?" Debbie asked, her voice trembling with fear.

"She didn't say," Evans replied as they approached the crosswalk.

They waited for the light to turn green. Evans turned to the kid.

"Danny, do you know what 'fall on your sword' means?"

From the look on his face, the kid was clueless.

"In your case, Danny, it means this: I made a terrible mistake. I'm sorry for what I did. I will never do anything like it again."

The light turned green.

"Let's go," Evans said.

****

The door opened and Mary Salazar came into the hallway.

"Mrs. Archer, Danny, please, come in," she said.

Danny stood up, trying to find strength in something Newman had told him a couple of days ago. *You'll make mistakes and pick plenty of bad waves. Learn what you did wrong and pick better ones. Oh yeah, what did Officer Evans tell me?*

"I'll wait out here," Evans said.

Debbie and Danny sat at a small conference table Mary had in her office. After picking up a file from her desk, she joined them. Mary Salazar was old school and somewhat of a tyrant according to her younger and more progressive colleagues. She left her smile in her car before she came to work, and, in her opinion, sympathy was a word in the dictionary somewhere after shit and suicide.

Holding up a piece of paper, she said, "This is the recommendation signed off on by the Juvenile Court judge."

By the callous manner in which she tossed it on the table, Debbie was sure Salazar disagreed with it. Then Salazar held up a couple of more pieces of paper.

"What concerns me," she added, "are arrest records of Joey Alders and Sammy Baker; your friends, friends you decided to hang around with, friends who convinced you it's ok to steal beer and smoke dope. I wonder what else they'll convince you to do?"

Before either Debbie or Danny could answer, "And then I get these," she added, holding up two additional papers. "One recounts a rather heroic deed you performed at a swim program for the Rec Department. The other is a letter from one of Santa Cruz's finest vouching for your character and asking for community service as a consequence for your stunt at the liquor store." Salazar leaned back in her char. "What to do?"

The three sat in silence for what seemed an eternity. Salazar leaned forward in her chair.

"Danny, this is the first time you've ever gotten into any kind of trouble with the law. How do I know it will be the last time?"

The saliva was gone from his mouth. His throat muscles had constricted to a point where breathing was difficult. He forced himself to look at Salazar.

"I did something ready bad. I know it and I'm awful sorry. I promise you I'll never do anything like that again."

Salazar looked at the boy. "I don't believe what I just heard. No excuse. No, they made me do it."

Danny straightened up in his chair.

"No ma'am. I decided to go along with them. That was a mistake I'll never make again."

Without so much as a smile, Salazar gathered up the papers in front of her and said, "Mr. Dinh is expecting you tomorrow around noon time. You'll be helping him for a couple of hours with whatever he needs help with for the next two weeks."

Salazar looked at Debbie. "You can take him home now, Mrs. Archer." Looking back at Danny, she said," If you were my kid, you'd get the whipping of your life."

When he stepped into the hallway, his lungs exploded as he gasped for air.

"Danny, do you realize how lucky you were?" Debbie asked.

"I do, Mom. I really do."

"I take it everything went alright?" Evans asked.

Debbie looked at him with that *you're not fooling me* look.

"Yes, thanks to a letter from Tara and a recommendation from one of Santa Cruz's finest. Any idea who that is?"

Bill Evans broke out into a smile. Had he looked at Danny's mother, he would have seen the same.

****

The remaining days of summer slipped by for Danny with scarcely a thought of the coming school year. Between his job at the swim program, his required time spent helping Mr. Dinh at the Seven-Eleven, and surfing in the late afternoon, starting the eighth grade at Holy Cross in less than a month was not on his mental landscape.

The surf that afternoon was exceptionally good. After sitting through what Danny thought was an eternity of small waves, they finally arrived--sets of really good waves, one after the other, came with unusual regularity. They started near the Point and didn't fade out until past the O'Neil house. After one last ride on a very fun wave, Danny made his way in to shore. He eased out of the top of his wet suit, letting it dangle at waist level, and headed up the steps.

"Nice out there, wasn't it?" asked Newman.

"Great," Danny said, slightly winded from toting his new surf board, a gift from Newman, up the flight of stairs.

"Summer's going to be over soon," Newman mused. His hands were clasped behind his head as he leaned back in his chair as if he were going to make some sort of grand pronouncement. Grand was not Newman's style, subtlety was.

"Yeah," groaned Danny, now realizing how close the start of the school year was.

"You know one of the things I love about surfing, Danny? The anticipation that the next wave will be the best one. And I've never been disappointed. Everyday has its best wave."

Danny hung his wet suit on the line in the backyard to dry, then hit the outdoor shower. He stopped outside the sliding door to his bedroom to make sure his feet were dry lest he face a scolding from his mother. When he looked on his bed, he saw them; brown corduroy pants, a short sleeve tan shirt and a maroon sweater. *Had to be the uniform*, he thought. The sight of it quickly erased any expectations of good things the priest and Newman had tried to build up.

****

Debbie had decided not to mention how good she thought Danny looked in his school uniform. The vanity of the preteen had already put Danny in front of his bedroom mirror too many times. He was sure he looked like a grape with brown legs.

"I made you scrambled eggs," Debbie said, when Danny appeared in the kitchen.

"With bacon?" he asked.

"Always," Debbie smiled. "Four slices just as you requested, Your Highness!"

Now he smiles. Thank God! She thought.

"I'm going to drive you today, Danny. According to Sister Agnes, there's some issue I need to clear up at the office. We'll need to leave a little early."

"Gee, I hope I never have her as a teacher," Danny said, shoving the last strip of bacon into his mouth.

Debbie didn't have the heart to tell him, but the school had mailed her Danny's class schedule. There it was, History—Sister Agnes. Telling him would only add to his anxiety.

"Don't get all worked up," Debbie said. "I'm sure you'll like all your teachers."

****

They pulled into the parking lot near the school office.

"Ok, when we're done, that's the building you go to," Debbie said, pointing to a large two story structure. Your class is the first one on the right." They headed into the office.

The receptionist, Mary Woodson, stood as she saw them enter. Debbie immediately had Danny take a seat.

"Don't tell me, first day jitters already?" she said.

"Oh, no," Debbie answered. "Sister Agnes said there was some issue with paperwork I needed to clear up today."

"I'll get her," the receptionist replied.

The hallway resounded with the echo of the taps Sister Agnes wore on her shoes. It was like some sort of sadistic warning she wanted you to hear. *I'm coming.*

"Mrs. Archer, please come with me," Sister Agnes said.

Danny stood, expecting he would have to come too.

"I said Mrs. Archer." The glare that flared from her eyes and the acid tone in her voice sent Danny into a virtual free fall in his chair.

Once in her office, Agnes handed Debbie her financial aid application.

"You won't be needing this," Agnes said.

Now it was Debbie's turn to panic.

"Sister, are you telling me my application for financial aid was rejected? I can't believe it. There's no way I can afford the tuition you charge and the uniforms I already bought." Debbie had both a sense of frustration and anger at hearing the Sister's words.

"No, Mrs. Archer, that's not what I mean," Agnes snapped. "You won't be needing financial aid because, according to Father Michael, someone has paid your son's tuition for the entire year. Anonymously, I might add."

The shock of this news caused Debbie Archer to slump back in her chair and gasp, "I don't understand, Sister Agnes."

"Well, apparently you have a secret benefactor, Mrs. Archer. Now, if you'll excuse me, I've got a lot of work ahead of me, what with this being the first day of school."

Agnes escorted Debbie out of her office and back to the receptionist. In the short time Debbie had been gone, Mary Woodson had befriended Danny. He was standing at the counter. Mary had a large binder opened and was explaining to Danny what classes he was going to take and who his teachers were.

"Here is your History teacher," Mary said, as Danny followed her finger across the page. His head dropped. *He saw Sister Agnes' name*, Debbie thought.

"This one you're really going to like," Mary said gleefully, trying to give the boy some measure of hope. "Miss Raye. She teaches Yoga and Health Science."

At the sound of Miss Raye's name, Agnes' face resembled that of someone who had been force fed concentrated lemon juice.

Her voice snorted, "There was a time when we focused on academics."

The receptionist gave Agnes a slight smirk, as if to say, of course, *your ancient Holiness!*

Agnes turned her attention to Danny. "It's your first day, don't be late, young man," she scolded.

Debbie managed to stifle what she really wanted to say and muttered, "Thank you, Sister."

Once outside, she gave Danny a hug, wished him well on his first day and headed to her car. The nun's caution hardly made Danny move fast. If anything, it only distracted him, as he walked across the parking lot, thinking how miserable History was going to be. The sudden blast of a horn, followed by a voice that shouted, "Move it, slow poke," startled Danny to the point he almost dropped his books. He hurried to the sidewalk, then stared back at his antagonist. The driver, a teenager, had slammed on the brakes of some sort of new model car.

"The next time be ready when the driver's ready. It's my time you're wasting," he chided the boy getting out of the passenger door. The boy slammed the car door shut, flipped the driver his middle finger, then spun around.

"Very funny, asshole," shouted the driver, as he sharply turned the car. That's when Danny noticed the surf board sticking out of the partially opened truck. Now Danny Archer might not have had a mind for remembering what his teachers said, but when it came to surfing and surf boards, his was a photographic memory. *Yeah*, he thought, *a bright blue Stormblade. I remember that one. Newman gave an etiquette lesson to the guy riding it after he ran into Fletcher.*

"What are you looking at!" challenged the boy who had just been called 'asshole'.

Danny said nothing. He eyed the boy as he walked up the steps. Danny wasn't afraid of him, but there was too much going on in his brain to react at that moment. He headed to the building Mary Woodson had pointed out to him. The door with the number eight above was his destination. When he walked in, he felt like he must have a horn growing out from the middle of his forehead. Every head turned to check him out, the new kid. To his eternal gratitude, there was an empty desk at the end of the first row.

****

Chapter 9

"Good morning, everyone," the priest said.

"Good morning, Father Michael," echoed the class of twenty-five eighth graders.

"After all these years, do I really need to correct you on my first name?" he grinned.

"No, Father Mike," chorused the class.

The subtle nod of recognition from the priest took some of the edge off Danny's anxiety.

"Let's begin with the Our Father," directed Father Mike.

Everyone rose. "Our Father who art in heaven…"

So began Danny Archer's introduction to Catholic education. By the end of the day, he had been exposed to the Hail Mary, the Apostles Creed, the Rosary, the Stations of the Cross, and most importantly, the Act of Contrition, if you were Catholic, that is.

"You've been blessed with a short day, today," Father Mike said, after the opening prayer. "The bookstore will be open until noon. After your teachers make their introductions, you are free to go. This is your last year at Holy Cross and then you'll be off to high school. Enjoy it. Learn from it and God bless each and every one of you."

"I'm Beni Andrews. That's Beni with an i not a y, Andrews. You're new here, aren't you?" the boy sitting next to Danny asked.

"Yeah," Danny replied. "I'm Danny Archer. I transferred here from Bay Elementary."

The boys shook hands. "You'll like it here for the most part," Beni whispered. "Most of the teachers are cool, except for Sister Agnes. And most of the kids are ok, except for him."

Beni pointed to a kid in the front of the class who had just pulled the kid in the first desk out of his spot.

"I sit here, turd," he said to the boy who was now picking himself up off the floor.

"His name is Garrett Collison. He's a jerk," Beni said, slightly under his breath.

Danny recognized him as the kid who had challenged him in the parking lot after flipping off the driver of the car he had arrived in. With no authority figure there, the volume of conversation between students began to rise, that is until Sister Agnes entered the room. Her appearance was followed by utter silence on the part of all students, except for Garret Collison, who continued his conversation with the girl sitting behind him.

"What makes him that way?" Danny asked.

"Money. And he thinks because he takes Karate he's the toughest kid in school. He's always looking to fight someone." Beni said.

"Mr. Collison, need I remind you to be quiet when you are in your seat?"

Collison faced forward as slowly as he could, showing the nun the maximum amount of defiance he could muster. Agnes approached the desk which sat upon a raised platform. She set her folder down, then picked up her attendance sheet. She ran her fingers down the list of names then looked at the class.

"Really everyone!" she said. "Are your memories so short you've forgotten how I arrange my class?"

She walked over to the first desk in the first row. "Mr. Archer, you sit here. Mr. Austin, behind Mr. Archer..." and so on until she had everyone arranged in alphabetical order. To Danny's delight, Beni Andrews sat across from him, and Garrett Collison assumed his rightful place in the last seat of the second row. When she was finished, Sister Agnes handed a stack of papers to each student in the front seats with instructions to take one packet and pass the rest to the rear.

"This is an outline of the material we will be covering in History this year. It lists homework assignments and when they're due, test schedules and the date your subject paper is due. Homework will be turned in timely. There is no such thing as a makeup test. Miss one and you'll lose credit points."

A hand shot up. "What's a subject paper, Sister Agnes?" Beni asked.

"Excellent question, Mr. Andrews," Agnes replied. "It will be a paper on a subject of your choosing in which you must explain its connection through History."

Andrews was sorry he'd asked.

****

Danny eyed the large clock on the wall. It's secondhand visibly hesitated at each second mark. At this rate, he thought, the half day Father Mike mentioned would easily feel as though it was lasting all day.

Unlike Bay Elementary, where Danny had one teacher for all his subjects, Holy Cross used four teachers for their 6th, 7th and eighth grades. It had been a hard sell for Father Mike when he came in as the new principal three years ago. A few of the newer staff, like Kelly Raye, newly hired health science and yoga instructor, embraced the concept. It gave them the time to hone their curriculum, as well as personalize it to each child's needs. But many of the older staff, religious and laity, fought father Mike tooth and nail. As Sister Agnes, who spearheaded the opposition to the change, so eloquently put to the Board of Directors, "the tradition of one teacher for each class, one teacher to monitor and evaluate all subjects, one teacher in charge must be maintained for the children's sake."

Fortunately, for the children, several of the eight-member board of directors were employed by high-tech companies springing up in the Santa Clara Valley. The classroom model that Sister Agnes stressed so passionately was exactly what they had bolted from in the business world; that lock step philosophy where one president had dictatorial control over every level of decision-making. The six-two vote was not unanimous, but it set the tone for what Holy Cross would become--a school of innovation.

Along with the schedule change, Father Mike introduced the concept of guest speakers for the eighth grade class. He explained to the board, "The idea is to use these individuals to show our students what real life jobs are about, and more importantly, to show them how what they've learned at Holy Cross applies to different professions.

****

"Hello everyone. Nice to see you again." The greeting from the Health Science and Yoga teacher, Kelly Raye, was in stark contrast to that of Sister Agnes.

"I'm not going to take much of your time, in case some of you want to hit the beach."

A round of applause greeted those words.

"No class handouts, Miss Raye?" Beni Andrews asked.

Raye started to laugh. "No, Beni with an i not a y. No handouts, no schedule of tests. I'd rather you be excited about learning, not frightened by what you're going to have to learn. See you all tomorrow."

Sister Agnes had started the day, and fortunately for Danny, it only got better. Sister Mary Johnson, Danny's English teacher, was freshly out of the credential program at San Jose State. She spoke of expression, emotion, descriptive language, instead of nouns, pronouns, adjectives. Danny was confused, but in a good way, not the way he had been during English class at Bay, he thought. Mr. Horton, his new math teacher, spoke of the calmness and confidence that came with the certainty of mathematics. No second-guessing, no wondering what if. When math gave you an answer, that was it. And then Ms. Raye. Overall, Danny Archer had not had such a bad day.

****

With his books in hand, Danny headed down the hill to catch the bus home. His new friend, Beni Andrews, tagged along. They had just passed the Vallarta Taqueria on Pacific when the boys heard it.

"Hey, wetback. No burrito today?"

Beni didn't bother turning around. He had heard it before from the same voice. Danny turned around to see Garrett Collison standing next to a car.

Danny recognized the blue surfboard sticking out of the open trunk of the car.

"Keep walking," Beni said, hoping Collison would ignore them.

Away from the watchful eyes of the staff at Holy Cross, Garrett Collison had found an extra measure of courage.

"Hey, wetback. I'm talking to you," Collison shouted, then he took a couple of steps and pushed Andrews from behind, causing him to stumble and drop his books.

It wasn't like Beni and Danny had become best friends, but Andrews was small for his age and Collison towered over him. The sneak attack provoked some sort of protectiveness in Danny. He stepped forward and pushed Collison in the chest. The bully fell against the car parked at the curb.

"Pick on someone your own size," Danny snapped.

"Well, you're about my size, asshole," Collison retorted, as he righted himself, then took a bladed stance, crossing his hands over each other in a circular motion. "I know Karate!"

"I don't care if you know the president of the United States," Danny shot back. There was a momentary pause while Collison decided what to do. Danny had already decided what he was going to do. He remembered Newman's words after he grabbed the young surfer who had run into his friend, Fletcher, that day. *I try to away from situations like that, but sometimes you can't. Especially if someone is getting hurt.*

Karate lessons had given Garrett Collison a false sense of confidence and superiority. His battles had always been in a gym and under the watchful eye of a dojo. Now, he was in a different world. Danny held his ground. He was waiting for the sign. From all his scrapes in the past, Danny had learned one thing. If he thought the other guy was going to swing at him, Danny swung first. Then it happened. Collison brought his hands up and over his head in a circular motion. When he did, Danny shot a right hand to Collison's stomach as hard as he could. As Collison bent over, Danny put him in a headlock with his right arm and with his left fist, he delivered several quick blows to Collison's face. Collison sank to the ground when Danny let go.

"What the hell's going on," came the shout from a young man approaching them. The shout not only startled Danny and Beni, it alerted the cop on a motorcycle who was witnessing the entire confrontation from across the street.

"He started it, Dalton," Garrett shouted to his older brother. "I was only trying to help Andrews get up when he swung at me for no reason."

Danny guided Beni behind him and whispered, "If something happens, run." Danny knew this time if something happened, it would be two on one.

"You start this?" The older brother demanded.

92

"Who's asking?" The defiance in Danny's voice was rising.

Dalton Collison was every bit the bully his younger brother was, and even more entitled by the family name, if that were possible.

Before he could answer, a voice said, "Boys, do we have a problem here?"

They turned to see a Santa Cruz policeman standing next to his motorcycle.

"My name is Dalton Collison. This is my younger brother, Garrett. You probably know my father Wilson Collison. He heads the Pacific Coast Stock Exchange."

"So I've heard," said the officer whose tone exuded more than a little contempt. Turning to the other two boys, he said, "Danny, how are you and your friend?"

****

"Newman, can I talk to you?"

Newman looked at his young friend and thought, *usually this type of question comes when he's done surfing, not before he's even gone out.*

"Sure kid, but then we're going surfing."

****

By the time his mother got home around five, the cathartic several hours spent with Newman and surfing had prepared Danny for what he thought was going to be the worst day of his life. When he passed Haws Ave, he saw the police car parked across from his house. *The bad news is here*, he thought. When he got to the driveway, he paused behind his mother's car. Peering over the back of the car, he saw his mom give the policeman a quick hug. It was the cop Danny had come to think of as a friend, Officer Bill Evans.

****

"So, had quite the first day at school, huh?" said his mom, adroitly putting some space between the officer and herself.

Danny took a deep breath and let it out slowly, something Newman had told him to do. "Honest Mom, it wasn't my fault. This one kid pushed a kid I was walking with to the ground and it was going to get worse unless I stepped in."

"Put your surf board down and come here," Debbie said. Oddly to Danny, it didn't sound like the coming of impending doom. He leaned his board against the palm tree in the front yard and walked up to the porch. Her arms went around her son. With loving approval, she gave him a long tender hug.

"Danny, Bill has offered to take us to Cole's barbeque, if it's alright with you? There is a little more to the story you need to know."

Cole's Barbeque was his favorite. But his heart was sending him signals his brain did not understand

****

After finishing his second large Coke, the inevitable partially stifled burp erupted. "Sorry," uttered a slightly embarrassed Danny.

Bill could only smile as Debbie dramatically rolled her eyes. It was Bill's cue.

"We all know Dalton and Garret's versions of what happened are different from yours. That's a given. So, based on their statements, Father Mike was forced to schedule a meeting with his father and your mother tomorrow."

Danny's shoulders slumped. "Whenever I do something wrong, there's a meeting."

Bill looked at Debbie whose eyes were welling up with tears at the sound of her son's defeatist voice.

"Danny," Bill said, putting his arm around the boy's shoulders. "You did the right thing in protecting your friend, but that doesn't mean there aren't consequences."

Danny raised his head. "That's what Newman told me once."

Evans smiled and started to laugh. "Well, he said the same thing to me years ago."

Beneath the table, Debbie squeezed Evans' hand. His smile grew.

Chapter 10

Debbie was intentionally early for their meeting. She was hoping to get a word with Father Mike before Wilson Collison arrived.

"Father Mike's not here yet, Mrs. archer. You and Danny can wait here," Mrs. Woodson, the receptionist said.

Debbie and Danny took their seats. Within minutes, the door to the office opened. Wilson Collison marched in with his sons in tow.

"Good morning, Mr. Collison. Father Michael's not in yet. You and your son can wait here."

The elder Collison ignored Woodson's directions. He looked at Debbie and her son with a menacing glare.

"No. I'll be in his office," he stated without equivocation. Down the hall they went.

****

The next five minutes seemed like an eternity until Father Mike arrived.

"Mr. Collison decided to wait in your office, Father," Woodson said to the priest.

Debbie stood up. "Do you want Danny and me to come with you, Father?"

Father Mike turned to her. "Debbie, I don't think that will be necessary. Let me speak with Mr. Collison alone."

Debbie's heart sank. *He's going to take their word for what happened and Danny will be expelled.*

Debbie's head rested against the wall. Her eyes stared upward to a picture of Jesus on the wall. Her eyes closed and a prayer was made. The sound of footsteps pounding down the hallway ended her supplication.

"You haven't heard the end of this, Father," Wilson Collison avowed.

The door slammed behind them. Debbie archer was beyond confused. *What the hell is going on.* The priest looked at Danny.

"Danny, can I talk to your mother first, then I'll talk with you?"

The boy nodded ok.

Once inside his office, Debbie asked quizzically, "What's going on, Father Mike?"

The priest smiled and pointed to some papers on his desk.

"These are the statements from Garrett and Dalton Collison. They read like they were written by a lawyer, which in fact, they probably were, some junior attorney on Wilson Collison's staff. This," he continued, pointing to another letter, "is the statement of Officer Bill Evans."

After she read the statements from the Collison boys, Father Mike handed officer Evans report to Debbie.

"After Wilson Collison read it, I told him he had two choices," Father Mike said. "Either he could drop this entire issue including his demand to have Danny expelled or I would be forced to bring this matter to the Board of Directors and they would have an opportunity to read Officer Evans' report."

Debbie Archer was at a loss for words.

"What did Mr. Collison mean when he said this isn't over yet?"

Father Mike leaned back in his chair.

"Well, I expect to find out that Wilson Collison's offer of a $100,000 donation to the building fund will be withdrawn. He will withdraw Garrett from Holy Cross and enroll him in some private school somewhere. He'll claim inadequate academic instruction and poor classroom control. Wilson Collison gave a lot of money to get Burke Preparatory

Academy in Aptos started so I imagine Garrett will join his brother Dalton there when he starts high school." The priest could see the look of concern on the mother's face.

"Not to worry Debbie, Father Mike said. "In fundraising you only count on what you have, not on what someone promises. Wilson Collison isn't the only source of deep pockets Holy Cross can call on.

Father Mike stood up. "Everything's going to be okay, Debbie. Would you mind sending Danny to see me?"

Danny took a seat in front of the priest.

"I know you're not Catholic, Danny, so what I'm going to tell you is probably something you've never heard of, but I know you will in your religion class. In the Bible, Jesus speaks of turning the other cheek. He talks about the meek shall inherit the earth. But there's also a part in the Bible where Jesus became so angry at the money changers working in the temple that he angrily turned over their tables, threw their money onto the floor and tossed them out of the temple. My point is this: even Jesus got mad."

"I'll bet his mother was mad at him for that," Danny said.

"I'm sure she was," said a very smiling priest. "You can bet there were consequences when he got home. There always are. Have a good day, Danny."

****

Eighth grade at Holy Cross was not easy for Danny Archer. For starters, there was the homework issue. At Bay Elementary, Danny only had one teacher assigning homework. At Holy Cross, he had five different teachers giving out assignments, and from the amount of homework he took home every day, it didn't seem to Danny that any of them were talking to each other about how much work each was assigning.

The rules of conduct were more regimented than anything Danny had experienced at Bay: stand up when the teacher enters the room. Sit down when told to do so. Stand up when you are called upon to answer a question. Sit down when you're finished. Always respond, "Yes, Father, No, Father. Yes, Sister, No Sister. Yes, Sir, No Sir, Yes, Ma'am, No, Ma'am." And then there were the prayers. Catholic or not, Danny Archer was expected to be able to recite on demand any of the endless prayers the Catholic Church had. The boy had lost count of exactly how many there were.

On top of everything, Danny was coping, and not well, with the burgeoning relationship between Officer Bill Evans and his mother. It wasn't that Danny didn't like him as a friend, but he already had a dad, or at least memories of a dad, and he wasn't prepared to have those memories erased. He was struggling to understand some things and accept others. Through it all, though, he had Newman.

****

An Indian summer had extended good weather into the first part of October. With each weekend

100

spent surfing, Newman learned more and more of the young boy's adjustments.

"She's impossible, Newman. It's like I can't do anything right in her classroom," Danny said after recounting his latest encounter with Sister Agnes.

"She's a tough one, that's for sure," Newman replied.

As they sat on the beach looking out to the surf, a particularly big and ugly wave started to form. It broke quick, and seemed to form several smaller waves at the same time.

"Man, that was ugly," groaned Danny.

Newman kept his eyes on the lone surfer with enough nerve to tackle the wave and get a decent ride out of it.

"See what he did?" Newman asked.

"Not really," Danny replied, refocusing his eyes on the surfer now paddling back out.
"He wasn't fighting the wave. He took what it gave him and made it work."

"You mean like Sister Agnes?" Danny asked pensively.

Good God. Maybe, just maybe, Newman thought.

"That's not the only pebble in your shoe, is it?" Newman continued.

Danny had taken a seat against the fence along the cliff line and was facing Newman. It kept the setting sun out of his eyes.

"No," he answered.

"Then what?" Newman asked.

"Not what," Danny said. "Who."

"Ok," Newman groaned. "How about complete answers."

"Officer Evans."

"Bill?" replied a surprised Newman.

"I think he's starting to like my mom," Danny said. "And what's worse, I think she likes him too."

If only Newman could have let out the roaring laughter forming in his lungs. He kept a somber face.

"It's not easy to think she's forgetting your dad's memory, is it?" he asked.

The boy simply shook his head. "And I'm not going to forget him either," Danny pronounced, as he got to his feet. His face frowned with determination.

Newman folded his note pad and stood next to Danny. The beauty of the setting sun skimming off the waves headed toward shore captivated them.

"Remember the first wave you ever rode on your own?" Newman asked.

"Are you kidding, you were with me. Sure I remember," replied Danny. "It was great. Just like you said it would be."

"And the time you hung five for the first time, remember that?"

Without realizing where Newman was taking him, Danny smiled and said, "How could I ever forget that!"

Newman put his arm around the boy's shoulder. He stared out to the sea.

"Inside your heart, there's a memory bank where you've deposited all the wonderful experiences surfing has given you and will continue to give you. It's a wonderful thing, Danny," Newman continued, "You never throw any of those recollections away. They're always with you."

Newman folded his chair and picked up his note pad. "Your mom's got a memory bank as well, Danny. Let her have a chance to add to it and give yourself a chance as well."

****

There was an uneasy awkwardness at the dinner table that night. Debbie had asked Bill to have dinner with them. Danny replied with shrugs, not words, to anything asked of him. There was a knock at the door.

"I'll get it," said Danny, seeing an opportunity to get away.

"Newman, what are you doing here?" Danny asked of his friend standing at the door.

"I brought something for you," the sage replied.

"Danny, don't be so impolite. Ask Newman to come in," Debbie called out from the dinner table.

"Mrs. Archer, Bill, nice to see you two again," Newman said.

"To what do we owe the pleasure of your company?" Debbie asked.

"Danny was telling me today about his struggles with Sister Agnes and I thought this might help," Newman, handling Debbie a piece of paper.

"What is it?" she asked.

"It's the Lord's Prayer in Latin," Newman said. "Could be just the surprise Sister Agnes needs to hear."

"Gosh, Newman, I don't know how to teach Danny a prayer in Latin," Debbie said.

"Well, I do," Evans chimed in.

Debbie looked at her dinner partner. "And just how did you come about learning the Lord's Prayer in Latin?"

"Who do you think bruised these knuckles with an 18-inch oak ruler more times than I want to admit?" Evans asked.

"You had Sister Agnes as a teacher?" Danny asked, stunned at the thought he and Evans had something in common.

"Yep. Seventh and eighth grades at Holy Cross."

"Well, that explains it," Debbie chuckled.

"Explains what?" Danny pleaded.

"Hatred of fish sticks," Evans said with a scrunched up face. "Danny, Sister Agnes was the strictest, must unreasonable, unbending teacher I ever had. I hated her. I took Newman's advice. Rather than fight her, I decided to give her what she wanted in a way she would never expect."

"What was that?" Danny asked, now fully attending to anything Bill Evans said.

Evans started. "I was having the hardest time in her class. She told me I needed to do some extra credit just to get a 'C'. When I told a friend about it, he suggested I learn to say the Lord's Prayer in Latin. I thought it was really a cool idea. All I had to do was find someone who could teach me the prayer in Latin."

"Did you find someone?" Danny asked.

"Yeah, I did," laughed Evans. "Believe it or not, the school secretary, Mrs. Woodson. She spent several years in a convent before deciding sins of the flesh were something worth exploring. I spent so much time in her office after school, my parents thought I was in trouble. And you know what? It worked. Old Agnes was floored when I recited the prayer in class. She gave me an 'A'."

"Do you think Mrs. Woodson would help me?" Danny asked, much to the amusement of everyone.

"You'll have to ask, young man," his mother said.

****

Chapter 11

"My goodness, Daniel Archer. It's been years since anyone asked me to teach them a prayer in Latin, but of course I will," Mrs. Woodson replied when Danny posed the question.

Twice a week, Danny would report to the school office where Mrs. Woodson would put him in a small room at the end of the building usually reserved for kids on detention. There she gave him small bits of the prayer to practice. For all the potential his test scores indicated he had, language proficiency was not one of them. Aside from the normal apprehension he felt just going to Sister Agnes's class, the tension of trying to learn Latin was taking its toll. Another one of Danny's teachers noticed the signs.

****

"Ok everyone. Roll up your mats and I'll see you next Monday."

Kelly Raye watched her last yoga class of the day stack their mats in the corner of the classroom.

"Danny, would you mind staying for a few minutes?" she asked.

"Yes, Ms. Raye."

His immediate first thought was he was in trouble. Raye recognized the look of "What did I do wrong now!" on his face.

"You don't need to worry. There's nothing wrong," she said. "I've been noticing you seem a little distracted in class lately. Is anything going on you'd like to talk about?"

"Not really," Danny said.

"Well, you know I'm here for you, right?" she asked.

Raye had a way of asking without seeming like she was prying into your inner self. She'd been dealing with kids like Danny for years. Some were difficult to lead to water, much less get them to drink. Archer was one of those. Allowing students to be different and recognizing all kids don't learn the same way were real strengths in her, strengths not always recognized by some of her peers, Sister Agnes in particular.

"Yeah, I know, Ms. Raye," Danny answered.

Raye also had another amazing quality. She knew if she gave a student the time to not have to say something, eventually, he or she would say something. It worked.

"I'm not sure talking about it would help," Danny said, pausing at the door of the classroom.

"If you try, I'll listen," she said.

His hesitation was her sign. She rolled out a couple of mats and sat on one. Danny followed her lead. Raye never once looked at the clock on the wall. She focused her attention on the young boy sitting cross legged next to her. Danny was having enough trouble in his History class with Sister Agnes, and now he was struggling to find a way to get in her good graces in her Religion class by learning the Lord's Prayer in Latin. It was all a little overwhelming for him.

"Sometimes when I know I have to go to her class, my heart feels like it's about to jump out of my chest," he said.

"You know, Danny, I feel the same way whenever I have to go to the dentist or deal with my ex," she said.

"What do you do?" he asked.

Raye explained to Danny the Yoga principle of Pranayama or breathing exercises.

"Within each of us, there's something called our life force. When we are in control of it, there's a sense of inner peace and tranquility. When we allow outside forces to control it, we are in a state of imbalance and that causes tension and anxiety. Sounds complicated, huh?" she asked.

"Sort of," Danny replied.

Raye smiled to herself. Father Mike had been partially successful in getting the Board of Directors to buy off on allowing Raye to teach Yoga. It was Raye who really got them to buy into on the concept. She told them Yoga was not intended to compete with traditional courses, but rather complement them. Yoga taught discipline, focus, internal control of emotions. "How many of you, when you were in school, had test anxiety and did poorly, even though you knew the material frontward and backward?" They agreed to one session a week. By the end of her first year, there was so much interest in her class, they allowed her to have two sessions a week.

"When you do have Sister Agnes' classes?" she asked.

"First and second periods," he answered.

She thought for a moment. "There's only so much I can cover in yoga class two times a week. If you're willing to come in say, fifteen minutes earlier each day, I'll show you some Pranayama exercises and some other yoga poses to practice. I know it will really help."

Danny hoped so as he nodded his head 'ok.'

****

"I miss these times," Newman said. "Can't wait for summer time so we can have more of them."

"Me too, Newman," Danny replied.

He attached his leash line to his ankle and paddled after Newman. Debbie had allowed Danny to surf early this Saturday as a reward for working so hard on his school work. Holy Cross wasn't allowing Danny to coast through his classes on potential. It was wearing on the boy.

"Are we ever going to surf?" asked an exasperated Danny after idling on his board for what seemed like an hour.

Newman straightened his legs and let out a deep breath.

"Do you know why I spend so much time here?"

"You mean surfing?" Danny asked.

"Not just surfing, but also sitting up on the cliffs."

Danny shook his head 'no.'

"When I'm out here or up there," he said, pointing to the cliffs, "I experience a certain calmness. I don't hear the waves. I don't hear people hollering. The motion of the water is like a sedative. It's like I'm being carried away to a place where there's no uncertainty, no distrust, no alarm."

"But you don't stay there, do you, wherever there is?" Danny asked.

Newman smiled and adjusted the cap of his wetsuit.

"How could I stay here?" he laughed. "But that calmness and peacefulness, I can take it with me to whatever I do next."

****

An already crowded schedule became even more hectic with Danny's afternoon lessons with Mrs. Woodson and early morning yoga sessions with Ms. Raye. Rather than crumble under the load, Danny Archer seemed to thrive.

"You see, Danny, it's not Sister Agnes that is the problem. It's the anxiety you feel. Breathe in, and let go of that anxiety and the problem goes away. She'll become just another teacher."

Danny was actually beginning to notice a difference. As he became more adept with the various Pranayama breathing techniques such as breath retention, channel cleaning and conquer breath, he began to experience a certain serenity. And as he began to hold his yoga poses like the bridge pose, the eagle pose and the child's pose, longer and longer, the tightness brought on by the stress and anxiety of thinking about Sister Agnes faded.

One day Ms. Raye dropped a bomb on Danny.

"You know, Danny, I never intended to teach you about breathing and yoga poses just to deal with your problem with Sister Agnes. What you've learned can be applied to relieve any fear, anxiety or tension no matter what the cause. It's more of a life philosophy than a situational cure."

Like a jigsaw puzzle, Danny was beginning to see the picture. It was still a little fuzzy in certain places. After all, all the pieces were yet to be put in place. The dots were there and connections were beginning to be made. *Newman and Ms. Raye were speaking the same language.*

****

This was his last session with Mrs. Woodson. Danny glanced down at the paper for the last time. The words had actually begun to have a certain flow to them.

Pater noster, qui es in coelis;
Sanctificatur nomen tuum:
Adveniat regnum tuum;
Fiat voluntas tua.

Sicut in coelo, et in terra.
Panem nostrum cotidianum da nobis hodie:
Et dimitte nobis debita nostra,
Sicut et nos dimittimus debitoribus nostris:
Et ne mos inducas in tentationem:
Sed libera nos a malo.

"Are you ready, Danny?" Mrs. Woodson asked.

"I am," he said confidently. He began, "Pater noster…" When he was finished, Mrs. Woodson had to dab the single tear rolling down her cheek.

"That was absolutely perfect," she sighed.

****

"Are you ready for today?" Debbie asked Danny that morning. Today was the day he was going to surprise Sister Agnes.

"Yes," Danny answered, as he glanced at a paper Ms. Raye had given him. It listed several breathing techniques and poses.

"Danny, isn't it more important that you be going over the Lord's Prayer instead that yoga stuff?"

"No, Mom. It's isn't. After I finish with Sister Agnes, this is going to continue."

There was no defiance in her son's voice. It was the quiet sense of confidence that surprised her.

****

Thanks to Sister Agnes's obsession with alphabetized order, Danny Archer was the first to be called on for everything. Being new to the school and a non-Catholic, his answers rarely set the bar very high for the next person. Today would be different.

"Shall we begin the extra credit assignments. Mr. Archer, would you please go first and please say what you are going to do?"

Danny stood up. "Yes Sister Agnes. I'm going to recite the Lord's Prayer."

There was no attempt to hide the laughter from many in the classroom who had been reciting the Lord's Prayer since the first grade. Even his friend, Beni, thought he had lost his mind. The look on Sister Agnes' face would have shot through him like a lightning bolt in the past. Not today though. Today, Danny Archer was in control. He began. You could have heard a pin drop as the Latin rolled off Danny's tongue as if it were a second language for him.

"Amen." He stood there, waiting to be told he could sit down.

She sat speechless. This time she was confused. She couldn't remember having ever heard such a recitation from one of her students, much less a non-Catholic student—take the Lord's Prayer, her favorite prayer by the way, and recite it in Latin. Perfect was a word Sister Agnes never, ever used. Her favorite archaic phrase was, "Nothing perfect can come from us who were born imperfect." Not today.

"Mr. Archer, I am more than surprised. That was as perfect a recitation of the Lord's Prayer in Latin as I have ever heard. Thank You. Please be seated." *It's been nearly twenty years since I heard a recitation like that,* she thought.

****

Chapter 12

"Hey, Ms. Raye," Danny Archer shouted upon seeing his favorite teacher at the grocery store known as Shoppers Corner. Raye pushed her cart to the side to allow another customer to pass.

"And how are you today?" she asked.

The grin on the boy's face prepared her to hear his good news.

"I got a 'B+' from Sister Agnes on my extra credit project. I couldn't have done it without your help," he said.

"Now that's something to be proud of young man. Sister Agnes is known to be quite stingy when it comes to handing out an 'A'," Raye replied.

"Yeah, I told her I was kind of hoping for an 'A'," Danny answered back.

"Wow, what did she say to that?" chuckled Raye.

"Actually she started to laugh," Danny said.

"Now I am surprised. She so stoic," chuckled Raye.

"Well, maybe not laugh actually, but she did smile," Danny said. "You know, Miss Raye, has anyone ever gotten an 'A' from her?"

"From what I've heard, no," she said. "I think her students give up because of the work involved. They're willing to settle for a B instead of putting out the effort and try for an A, you know what I mean?"

Oddly he did – Newman's words were resonating in his brain.

****

"Danny, are you sure you don't want to come?" Debbie asked.

"Is he coming?" Danny replied, referring to Bill Evans.

Debbie Archer had not yet had that "Come to Jesus" meeting with her son over her relationship with the policeman. Yes, there had been the makings of some sort of connection with Bill and Danny about Sister Agnes, but this was different. Thank God Bill understood.

"Debbie, please don't apologize about Danny," Bill had said that the last time they had a private moment. *"First, he lost his father. Now he sees me as a threat to take you away from him. He needs time."*

Her feelings erupted with more emotion than she wanted to show.

"How much time before I get to care again, Bill?" She asked.

"You already do, don't you?" He said, his arms pulling her to him.

Her whispered "yes" caused his arms to pull her closer. "This isn't about you caring, it's about Danny. He has to see your happiness is coming from caring for someone new and most importantly, he has to be happy someone new cares about him."

****

"No, sweetheart," Debbie said, glancing at her son. "The time we take to visit your father's grave is just for you and me."

Debbie purchased a bouquet of flowers at the cemetery gift shop. Then she and Danny headed to her husband's grave site. They stood before the headstone for the longest time before Debbie put the flowers in the conical shaped flower holder.

"What are you thinking, Mom?" Danny asked.

"Oh, Danny, I have such wonderful memories of your dad and our lives together that it breaks my heart when I realize they'll be no more."

Danny hugged his mother. Debbie had never provided Danny with any type of religious training. It wasn't like she or her husband didn't believe in a God. God was just there and they were here.

"I'm going to say a prayer to my dad," Danny said.

The confluence of his mother's words and Newman's advice caused more of a fog than clarity in the boy's brain. He hadn't quite connected the dots, but he was on his way. Suddenly, there was a new emptiness in the pit of Debbie's stomach.

"I'm so sorry, Danny, that I never taught you how to pray, or to whom," she said.

"Don't worry, Mom. Sister Agnes did. You can say the words after me. Our Father..."

****

If the emotional roller coaster of a young girl entering womanhood is the bane of parenting, the silent, moody withdrawal of an adolescent boy isn't far behind. Like a bear in hibernation in the deep of winter, his response to a question was an inevitable grunt. An answer of four words would be cause for a trip to the emergency room. Such was the state of mind for Danny Archer as Christmas vacation approached.

****

"I think you should talk to him, Bill," Debbie said over lunch. "Maybe he'd open up to you?"

Bill Evans had no doubt developed a fondness for the boy, but like a good attorney, he knew to never ask a question he didn't know the answer to.

"There's still a lot of unchartered territory between us," he answered. "Though there is someone he might open up to. I'll do some checking."

****

It was Saturday and Evans first stop was the cliffs where 36th Ave. meets East Cliff Drive. No Newman. Okay, plan B. Evans headed to the priest house at Holy Cross.

"Bill, gosh it's been a long time. Come on in. Coffee?" Asked father Mike.

Evans had noticed the priest's surfboard in the back of his truck and a wetsuit stuck under it.

"Mike, if you're headed to the beach, we can make this another time," Evans said.

Father Mike adjusted his pony tail and said, "Yes, I'm headed to the beach. No, we can talk now and what about that coffee?"

"Pour." Evans took a seat in the kitchen. Bill brought his friend up to speed about Danny's behavior and Bill's budding relationship with the boy's mother.

"You know any number of variables could come into play here, Bill. How can I help?"

"Have you heard any of the teachers express concern about Danny?"

No, not from the religious side of the house. If anything, they speak well of the boy—particularly Sister Agnes. It seems Danny's recitation of the Lord's prayer in Latin really moved her and that's not easy to do."

"How about the lay teachers? Evans asked.

"Same there, Bill," the priest said. "But on second thought, I know Kelly Raye has been spending extra time with Danny. She may know something."

"How can I get ahold of her?" Evans said, as he took out a small notepad from his pocket.

"If you've got the time, follow me. She's kind of a regular at this spot on Saturday mornings," father Mike said.

"Lead the way, Kemo Sabe."

****

It was anything but warm when the priest pulled into a parking spot above the cliffs at Capitola. Evans pulled in next to him. The temperature was in the mid-60s. The skies were overcast and somehow kept the offshore winds from kicking up the surf. It was the type of day the locals liked. No tourist dared the water because of the cold and the clouds. Father Mike and Evans crossed the street and stood next to the guardrail. The priest scanned the ocean.

"There she is," he said, pointing to a standup paddle board rounding the tip of the pier. "Let's go."

The two worked their way down the narrow sidewalk and then meandered through a maze of vacation rentals until they got to the beach. Raye waved to them as she untied her leash line and picked up her paddle board.

"Father Mike, going to try Cap today?" She asked.

"No, I'm headed to Cowells, but there someone I want you to meet. Kelly Raye, this is Bill Evans, a long-time friend. Bill, Kelly Raye."

The two shook hands.

"Say, you wouldn't be the famous Bill Evans who recited the Lord's prayer in Latin, would you?" Andrews asked.

His cover blown, Evans sheepishly said, "Yes. Damn, I thought my secret would stay hidden forever."

Raye started to laugh "Hardly, I was helping Danny with some pre-sister Agnes anxiety when he told me Mrs. Woodson was helping him. One thing led to another."

"Secrets, Bill? I'm shocked and appalled," the priest said mockingly. "Do you have time, Kelly, to talk to Bill about Danny Archer?"

"Sure. Do you mind if we go to Zelda's?" she asked.

****

The waiter delivered three glasses of Guinness. Glasses were tapped and the layer of foam on all three practically disappeared instantly.

"It's a good thing they can't talk," Raye said, nodding to a row of a half a dozen seagulls perched on the handrail, eager for some morsel of food to be thrown their way.

"What do you need to know about Danny Archer?" Raye asked, turning her attention back to the priest and his friend.

Evans explained everything to her. Raye had a most unique quality as a teacher. She not only taught kids, she allowed herself to learn from them.

"I can't shed any light as to the dynamics between you, Danny, and his mother," she said. "However, Sister Agnes is something else." Evans looked at Father Mike, then back to Raye. "How so?"

Kelly took a sip of her Guinness. "I may have created something of a monster in Danny archer."

The priest and the cop sat spellbound, as she told her story

"Danny knew he had nailed his assignment from Sister Agnes with his recitation, but when he got a 'B+', he was disappointed. He really expected an

'A'. He asked me if Sister Agnes ever gave anyone an 'A'. I told him I didn't think so because most of her students never wanted to put in the work she demanded, and frankly, Father, some of her demands are a little unreasonable. Just an observation, not a judgment" Raye said.

"Understood," said Father Mike, who had spent countless futile conversations with Agnes over the benefits of a taste of success versus a bucket of missing the mark.

"Anyway, Sister Agnes's project for her history class has got Danny in a tailspin," she continued. "It has to be an in-depth paper on a topic personal to you that you can trace through history. The paper must be unique and creative."

"By whose standard?" Evans asked.

"Ah, therein lies the rub, as Shakespeare would say," Raye replied, tipping her glass to Evans. "You see, Danny wants an 'A' on this project, but somehow Sister Agnes has become a challenge to him, one I'm not sure he wants to face. I don't know if there's anything in Danny's life that has challenged him quite the way Sister Agnes has. Deep down inside, I think Danny has a fear of failure in her class, to be held up just like everyone else, incapable of being the best, no matter how much work he does."

"It's not about being the best," Father Mike said. "It's about trying your best."

"Touché," replied Andrews.

****

Evans drove one more time by the O'Neil house. *Great, he's there.*

"Hey, Newman, don't go anywhere," Evans called out his passenger window. Newman waved. Evans found a parking space about four blocks away.

"Shit, Newman, even on a day like today, I can't find a place to park," Evans complained when he finally got back to Newman's location.

"Yeah, but the locals get a chance where the faint of heart wouldn't venture."

Unlike the surf at Capitola, the waves at Pleasure Point were unusually large and unpredictable.

"Man, I hate to be out in that mess," said Evans.

"Most people wouldn't," agreed Newman.

"Newman, I'm worried about Danny Archer."

"What now?" Newman said, putting his note pad aside.

Evans told him of his conversation with Father Mike and Kelly Raye.

"Debbie's concerned, as are Father Mike and Raye. The stumbling block seems to be Sister Agnes," Evans concluded.

"You're wrong, Bill," Newman said, matter-of-factly. "She's not the stumbling block, Danny is. Agnes is like the surf out there today—tough, unforgiving and frightening. How many times have you tackled a scary wave and been unceremoniously dumped on your ass?"

"Hell, Newman, more times than I want to count."

"Me too," Newman smiled.

"Ouch! That had to hurt," Evans said, as they watched a wave separate a surfer from his board. He disappeared under a cascading wall of water, his board soaring 20 feet in air.

"Bill, Danny's only problem is he is twelve years old, with virtually no life experience and no confidence as to how good he can be."

"Well, Newman, we don't have much time to teach him. Christmas vacation is just around the corner and his history paper for Sister Agnes is due when he gets back, and he hasn't even started."

"I'll try."

****

Chapter 13

"He's here, honey," Debbie said to her son. "Don't forget your lunch and a jacket. It could get windy."

Newman knocked on the door.

"Coming," Danny hollered. "Bye Mom."

Newman had called Debbie and asked if it would be okay to take Danny to a surf contest being held up the coast. Bill had told her of his conversations with Father Mike and Raye. He assured her if Newman was getting involved, it was good.

"Where to?" Danny said, as he shut the car door.

"Up the coast past Davenport. There is a Nor-Cal amateur surfing contest being held there. I thought you might enjoy it."

"Are you kidding!" Danny beamed.

Once in the parking area, Newman took a pair of binoculars and the backpack containing lunches and waters, while Danny toted two folding chairs. Newman insisted they get there early so they could get the best place to sit on the bluffs.

"Know how this works?" Newman asked.

"No," Danny said, his head pivoting in all directions at once, taking in the sights of arriving contestants and spectators.

Just then a horn blasted. It was 8 AM sharp and nearly 25 surfers began to battle their way through a series of crashing waves to the lineup point.

Newman's focus was on the surfers, and through his binoculars he could identify them by the colored sashguards they wore over their wetsuits.

"The judges are looking at a number of factors: how difficult is the wave, how hard are the maneuvers the rider takes, how creative is the rider with his maneuvers and the variety of maneuvers he uses."

"Sounds complicated," Danny said, as he used his binoculars to track the contestants.

"It's not really," Newman said. "Every surfer knows in order to win he has to challenge the biggest wave that comes his way. He's got a mental picture of what maneuvers he wants to try, but always in the back of his mind is how he could do this move or that move a little differently."

The two watched the first few surfers work a set of waves. Newman saw it coming, an unusually large wave. He alerted Danny.

"Be ready," he said. "Keep your eyes on the next wave and who takes it."

Danny strained his eyes to catch every detail while Newman provided the narrative.

"See how he rides the middle of the wave, not shooting to the bottom? Now watch him work up and down the midline. Those are sharp turnouts, Danny."

The wave was starting to curl. Newman knew what the rider was going to do.

"Watch him, now Danny. He's going to shoot the curl."

Danny's mouth dropped as he watched the rider step forward to the end of his board. He crouched down as the force of the wave pushed him through the tunnel of water formed by the curl.

"Wow, do you think I'll ever be able to do that?" Danny asked in amazement.

"If you take the toughest wave, work it as best you can, then yes, I think you could do that someday," Newman replied.

The rest of the day was pretty much the same thing. Newman would describe the difficulty of the wave, what maneuvers the riders would try and how well they performed.

"It's all about the wave, Danny, never forget that. When you're presented with a big wave and you don't try, if you give up because the wave looks too hard, too fast, whatever, you'll be a 'could have been' the rest of your life.

Newman wasn't going to chance that Danny might bring up the issue with his History project, so Newman did. Once back on the highway after the competition, Newman asked, "How's that project for Sister Agnes going?"

"How'd you know about that?" Danny asked.

"I know about a lot of things, young man, so how's it going?"

"It's not, Newman. I can't come up with an idea. Most of the guys are doing stuff about sports. You know like their favorite player. I just can't think of anything that's..."

"Unique and creative?"

"Yeah," Danny said dejectedly. "What do I know about unique and creative."

More than you think kid, if you'll only listen.

"Let's start with the basics," Newman said. "What do you love to do?"

"Surf," came the unequivocal answer.

"Ok then, let's talk about surfing."

Danny's curiosity was beginning to peak.

"Like a project on the history of the surf board?"

Before Newman could respond, Danny rejected his own idea. "No, it probably won't go back far enough in history for Sister Agnes. I think she wants us to go really far back in history."

Now you're on the right track.

"Well, if not the surf board, how about the wave itself."

"I don't get it, Newman."

"Like you said, the history of the surf board probably doesn't go back far enough, but the wave is something else. Do you know what the ancient Romans and Greeks or any other cultures, thought about the wave?"

"Here's another idea. Think of the wave as something other than water, like energy. You could start out with the idea of a water wave and wind up talking about other kinds of waves. Now that's creative," Newman said with a chuckle.

"Jeeze Newman, that sounds awfully tough."

"Maybe, but you saw today what happens to surfers who shy away from tough waves."

"But that's surfing, Newman. I'm talking about Sister Agnes," Danny sighed.

Whoops, back slide!

"Ok, who's to say the same solution can't apply to completely different problems?" It was Newman's best comeback, though he knew Danny needed a more direct answer.

"Look, go to the library and ask for the reference section. Go through the encyclopedia and check out the Roman Empire, and Ancient Greece. See what you can find out about waves. You can figure out the rest."

****

"Can you show me where the encyclopedias are, ma'am?" Danny asked the librarian at the main branch of the Santa Cruz Library.

"What, specifically, are you looking for?" she replied.

Danny explained his assignment to her.

"I think I have just what you're looking for. Come with me," she said.

Thanks in part to a grant from UC Santa Cruz, the main library research computers had a fairly sophisticated system. The librarian typed in several references.

"This will only take a second," she said, as she hit the print button.

A second it was. She handed Danny a piece of paper with several sites to check out.

"This should keep you busy for a little while," she said with a smile.

"A little while" was an understatement. Danny had told his mom he only needed to be at the library for an hour or so. When she stopped by to pick him up, he pleaded for more time. One reference led to another. He didn't know where to stop. Two hours later, Debbie returned.

"You've got to be done by now," she said.

"I think so, Mom, but I'll need help putting this all together. There's a ton of stuff here. Newman was right," he said, an edge of excitement in his voice.

Danny didn't need quite the help he thought he would from his mother. She monitored his progress, but pretty much, Danny did all the work. He asked her to look it over when he was finally finished.

"Wow, I never expected it to end that way," she said.

Danny didn't bother to contain his feelings. He laughed and smiled at the same time.

"Creative and unique, that's what Sister Agnes wanted and that's what she's going to get," he said, feeling highly pleased with himself.

****

The nuns' residence was an old Victorian across the street from Holy Cross Church. The sisters had finished their evening meal and most retreated to their rooms, except for Sister Agnes and Sister Mary. They headed to a conference room off the main living room. Agnes had a stack of projects in front of her chair. Sister Mary was correcting the last of several essays she had to grade.

"My Lord, if I have to read another paper about the history of some sports figure, I'm going to throw up," Sister Agnes groaned.

"Young boys have very narrow minds," said Sister Mary.

"Oh, it's not just the boys. Do you have any idea how many girls turned in papers on the feminist movement?

Mary knew she didn't need to respond.

"Agnes, I'm done with my work. Let me give you a hand reading some of those."

"Bless you," Agnes said. "Take your pick."

Mary did and she wasn't disappointed. This writer traced the history of the wave starting with the Greek Goddess of waves, Cymopoleia and the Roman belief that waves grow larger and larger in a series up to the largest wave, the ninth wave. He even noted the twelfth wave of consciousness in the Mayan culture. He certainly did his research, Mary thought. She was becoming the student and the author was her teacher. She loved the ending.

"The history of the radio wave and amber waves of grain are for another paper."

Sister Mary smiled to herself. *This could be the one.*

"Anything that looks like 'A' quality?" Mary asked, as Agnes put the last of the projects on a pile. Her fatigue had noticeably sapped her enthusiasm.

"Are you kidding?" she sighed.

Sister Mary handed her the paper she had just read. "Then you'd better read this and be prepared to be surprised," she said.

****

Chapter 14

After that first day of school and the subsequent transfer of Garret Collison to some private school in Santa Clara, Danny Archer earned a certain type of reputation. When Sister Agnes handed back everyone's project, his reputation went to a new level: the only student to ever get an 'A' from Sister Agnes.

****

With the start of the last semester of his eighth grade, a different Danny Archer appeared. He wasn't so intimidated by the work his teachers assigned. He wasn't as anxious or tense about things that used to bother him. Debbie knew the change was permanent when the subject of high school came up. Tuesday night at Cole's had become something of a tradition for Debbie Archer, Danny, and Bill Evans.

"Guess you have a decision to make," his Mom said. "Santa Cruz High or Harbor High, which is it going to be?"

It was a good thing her last bite of meat was a small one and that the last of Evans' beer was a swallow, or they both would have certainly choked to death on hearing Danny's answer.

"Actually Mom, I was thinking about taking the test for Burke Preparatory Academy."

Edmund Burke Preparatory Academy was an expensive private school where the wealthy sent their kids. Burke had the reputation of getting one hundred percent of their graduates into four year schools, and not any four year schools. They boast of the Ivy League, Stanford, and Northwestern, as landing places for their graduates.

"My God, Danny. Do you have any idea what it would cost to go there?" Debbie exclaimed.

"Sure," Danny said. "Father Mike said if I do well enough on the entrance exam, I could quality for financial aid to cover the tuition."

Debbie Archer's reservations went deeper than concerns about money. She knew the types of families that sent their kids to Burke. They were entitled and superior to others. A Cardio surgeon from Dominican, Dr. Gaylord Winston, sends his kids there. As a surgeon, he had no equal, but he was devoid of any sense of compassion for anyone whose income didn't have a minimum of three commas. Their kids drove fancy cars and wore expense clothes. How was she supposed to complete with that on her salary?

"We'll talk about this," Debbie said, her way of postponing a difficult and disappointing decision.

****

"What can you tell me about Burke Preparatory, Father Mike?" Debbie Archer asked. Since Danny had already had a conversation with the priest, he was a good person to start with.

"A very challenging curriculum, an excellent staff and recently, a strong push for diversity among their enrollment," he said.

The look of apprehension on her face told the priest he needed to asked some questions.

"You're concerned about how Danny will fit in, aren't you?"

"Some wealthy families send their children there, Father Mike. I just don't know if Danny's a good fit with those kind of people."

"Well, Debbie, Danny will be going to school with the children, not their parents. and yes, before you say it, some apples don't fall far from the tree, but others do. Try not to judge everyone by what you may have heard."

"I'm sorry, Father Mike. It's just that I drive an old car. I work as an LVN in a hospital where some fathers work who had their kids in Burke, and we hardly live in an upscale area."

"So who do you think won't fit in, you or Danny?"

Suddenly, Debbie Archer felt very uncomfortable.

138

"Guess I've been a little judgmental, both of them and myself,"

The priest smiled. *Yes, you have.*

"But there's still the matter of tuition," Debbie said.

"Burke Prep had a rather large endowment, a portion of which is used for families who can't afford the tuition and if a child does well on their placement test, they increase the amount of financial aid. Guess what one of Danny's strengths is, or have you forgotten?"

Yes, the test, any test. Debbie began to feel a little better.

****

After another conversation with Bill, Debbie thought she should talk with Newman. He'd been around Santa Cruz forever and he seemed to really understand Danny. Debbie decided to walk to the cliffs by the O'Neil house. She was in luck, Newman was there.

"Mind if I interrupt what you're doing?"

Newman glanced up from his notepad. "Why no, Debbie. I was just about to stop anyway. What's up?"

She explained how Danny had decided he wanted to go to Burke Preparatory. Father Mike had filled her in on the financial costs and how to deal with it. But she was still unsure.

"You know, Newman, it never occurred to me that Danny would want to go to a place like Burke Prep. It's a private school, high standards, and demanding class work. I just don't understand," she said.

She may not have understood, but Newman did.

"He saw the wave and he wants to ride it," he said.

"Ok, you'll have to explain that one," Debbie replied quizzically.

Newman stood up and walked to the handrail. "When Danny looks out at the surf, he sees waves, small waves, big waves, dangerous waves. I don't think Danny is afraid anymore of big, dangerous waves. He knows he won't ride out every wave, but he's no longer afraid to try. Maybe you shouldn't be either."

****

Debbie Archer was hardly superstitious, but when Danny returned from taking the placement test for Burke Prep, she didn't raise the question as to how he thought he did. She didn't want to jinx things. Danny was not so secretive.

"You know, it's ok to ask how I did, Mom."

With the ok to show her feelings, she threw the dish towel on the counter and said, "So tell me. I can hardly contain myself."

"Well, it was hard. But nothing that having Sister Agnes and Ms. Raye didn't prepare me for. I think I did good, Mom."

She gave her son a hug. He was growing up before her very eyes and suddenly she missed the little boy he used to be. Tears came.

****

In the ensuing weeks, there was a lot of good news for the Archer family. Danny's placement scores were exceptionally high. Along with a letter of acceptance came the application for financial aid. On top of that, Danny's new friend from Holy Cross, Beni Diaz, and Danny's old friend from Bay Elementary, Fletcher Williams, would be joining him at Burke. Burke would not be without challenges, in the classroom and elsewhere. What Danny Archer would have to deal with would affect him for the rest of his life.

****

Part II

Chapter 15

"Fred, I can't thank you enough for arranging this," Newman said.

"Yes, thank you so much," Debbie Archer added.

Danny stood silent at her side, somewhat in awe of the expansive campus that lay before him. His friends Fletcher and Benny were equally awed.

"Nervous?" His mother asked.

Newman answered for the boy. "He's checking out the waves."

Danny looked up with a smile on his face. Fred Wyckoff had arranged for a private tour of Burke preparatory Academy during the summer break. *Less intimidating*, he thought.

"So, this is Edmund Burke Preparatory Academy, founded in 1938 by a small group of wealthy businessmen who felt all the exclusive prep schools were located on the East Coast. They wanted something on the West Coast. Their intentions were to keep it small, so currently, there are about 1500 students. Most of them live on campus in residence halls we'll see later. Walk this way."

The founding fathers of Burke Preparatory Academy were not original thinkers as far as Newman was concerned. The sharply manicured lawns, ivy-covered brick buildings and 8-foot ornately designed wrought iron wall which surrounded the campus were a throwback to any of the dozen or more prep school designs on the East Coast.

Wyckoff took his charge through the two classroom buildings which faced each other, forming what the students referred to as "The Quad."

"How come there are no rows of desks in the classrooms?" Danny asked.

"We want our students to face each other and the teacher, so we arrange the desks in a circle," Wyckoff replied.

After touring the residence halls which looked to Debbie Archer like something out of the Embassy Suites, what with their two two-person bedrooms and a shared living area, they wound up back at Fred's office.

"So, Dean of Student Affairs and head of the Faculty/Student Council. Quite a load there," Newman said.

"It can be," Wyckoff replied. "Frankly, there are times when I wonder who's in charge, the faculty or the parents."

Danny looked at him. "Like taking a big wave, Mister Wyckoff?"

The adults smiled, no one more than Newman. But behind that smile, Newman was concerned. In the parking lot, Newman said, "Don't wait on me. Fred and I have to do some catching up."

Debbie drove off with the three boys.

"Beer?" Newman asked.

"Thought you'd never ask," Wyckoff replied with a smack of his lips.

****

"Thanks, Joe," Newman said to the bartender at the "Sticky Wicket," a bohemian type bar hidden away in Capitola. Joe sat two ice cold bottles of Budweiser in front of the men.

"To you," Newman said, tapping the tip of his bottle on Wyckoff's.

In silence, both savored that first cold swallow.

"So what exactly did you mean back there when you said sometimes you wonder who's in control?" Newman asked.

"Know what the tuition at Burke runs a year?" Wyckoff asked

Newman shook his head "no".

Wyckoff replied, "$15,000 a year and another $5,000 if you live on campus. For the first 30 years or so, old money and even older thinking influenced everything the Board of Directors tried to do."

"Such as?" Newman asked.

"Imagine the battle when the concept of making Burke coed came up, or when there was the initial discussion about a campaign to get more minority students enrolled. You'd have thought the North had fired on Fort Sumter all over again."

"The white way is the right way!" groaned Newman.

"Exactly," said Wyckoff, reaching for his beer. "Anyway, when the moneyed children of the Silicon Valley pioneers started arriving at Burke, the battle was on. It took several years before enough of the new blood got on the Board of Directors to make a difference. Even at that, the vote was always 8 to 7, one way or the other."

"Somehow I think you really have two battles— the parents and the apples that don't fall far from the tree," mused Newman.

"If you only knew," Wyckoff said. "You know, Newman, it's one thing to try and teach young people the difference between right and wrong, good and evil, but when the size of the parent's stock portfolios is the deciding factor, all hell breaks loose."

"And the worst of the old money is…?" Newman asked.

"Easy, that would be the great-grandson of Arthur Pennington III, founder of the Pacific Coast Stock Exchange, one Wilson Pennington Collison. He's taken the phrase' the world is my oyster' quite literally."

People like that have long memories and that won't bode well for Danny Archer, Newman thought.

"Here, I meant to give these to the boys before they left," Wyckoff said. He handed him three copies of a biography on the life of Edmund Burke.

"Tell them to read these before school starts. Incoming freshmen get them the first day of school. It will give them a leg up."

Newman took the books under his arm. "Places to go, things to do," he said.

Wyckoff chuckled at his old friend, thinking, *He's got no place to go but the cliffs at Pleasure Point and nothing to do but watch the surf.* How wrong he was.

****

"You need to read this," Newman said. "And remember what you read," he added for emphasis.

Danny flipped through the pages. "What is it?" he asked.

"The Life and Times of Edmund Burke," Newman replied. "It will come in handy when school starts, trust me."

Newman handed Danny a hot chocolate. "Here. It will help take the chill off."

Danny cupped his hands around the chocolate to smell the aroma. "Are we surfing later?"

"Not today. Today is a watch day," Newman said.

"Watch what?" Danny asked.

"I wanted you here early today to see how the bottom looks at low tide," Newman replied. He pointed to his right. "See that sand bar?"

Danny strained his eyes. "Yeah, I think."

"Ok. Now pay attention. In the winter time, sandbars are usually formed farther out. In the summer time, they're formed closer to shore. Whenever you're going to surf a new spot, check it at low tide and try to see when sandbars may be forming. The location can change all the time. Waves that are formed over sandbars are called 'Beach breaks'. Got it?" Newman asked.

"I will when I get a little more practice," Danny said.

"So let's practice," Newman responded.

At least two to three times a week, Newman took Danny to various surfing spots up and down the coast, sometimes at low tide, sometimes at high tide. Always the lesson was the same: spot possible locations of sandbars. Danny learned the three types of wave breaks, the reef break, the beach break, and the point break. Newman talked about how the unseen topography of the ocean floor influenced the type of waves that would appear.

"Whenever you go to any new place, say to surf," Newman said, "pay attention to where the waves break. Study them to see if the wave is contiguous or if there are break points. Watch those already in the water. See how they adjust to the waves. Know the ocean floor, if you can. Everything you can learn from the place and the waves will help you decide when to take it, when to break out, when to ride it for all it's worth."

Danny, Fletcher and Beni stepped off the bus at the bottom of Hillcrest Drive. They had a two block walk to their new high school. Hillcrest Drive dead-ended right in front of Burke Prep. To the right, directly across the street from the campus entrance, was the student parking. The expensive foreign cars, like BMWs and Jaguars, to American cars, like Corvettes and Lincolns, were an indication of the moneyed families whose children attended Burke. There were a number of painted signs with arrows

148

pointing where to go if you were a freshman, sophomore, junior, or senior.

"This way," said Andrews, pointing to a sign reading "Freshmen Orientation-Main Hall."

Danny and Fletcher dutifully followed. Danny walked the slowest, taking in every detail of the new place he was entering. It was not just the buildings and grounds he paid attention to; he also watched the student arrivals. Those who moved rapidly through the maze of sidewalks, laughing as they went, had to be returning students, he thought. Those who walked slower and with heads continuously turning had to be fellow freshmen like himself.

"Freshmen, please go inside and take a seat."

Danny recognized the man as Fred Wyckoff, Newman's friend who had taken them on a tour earlier in the summer. Like salmon swimming upstream, a steady flow of white shirts and khaki pants passed through the doors of Burke Hall. For the entire morning, the incoming freshman class listened to speakers talk about the history of Edmund Burke, the physical layout of the campus, building names, and everything else new students needed to know. Most of the freshmen were on sensory overload, save for one, Danny Archer. He was learning about the new place and soaking in everything he heard. Fred Wyckoff stepped up to the microphone.

"My name is Fred Wyckoff. I am the Chairman of the Faculty-Student Conduct Committee. This committee serves a very important role at Burke. The committee is composed of five faculty members and four seniors. The honor code of Burke Preparatory is something we as faculty take seriously, and you as students should do so as well. When students are brought before it for alleged violations, it is the role of this committee to determine the guilt or innocence of the student and the resulting consequences. The honor code is on the last page of the pamphlet you were given when you came in. Read it, know it, and live it accordingly. You are now released for lunch."

The freshmen were then directed to the dining hall.

"Wow," muttered Fletcher Williams, as he entered the dining hall.

The twenty-foot high walls of dark walnut panels had pictures of all the faculty, famous graduates, and numerous quotes attributed to Edmund Burke. Danny followed Fletcher and Beni along the cafeteria line, grabbing anything that looked good. Beni had found three empty chairs at the end of one table.

"Not too shabby, uh?" he asked.

"I'll say," answered Fletcher. "What do you think, Danny?"

"I think there won't be a lot of time to talk at lunch time," he said.

Fletch and Beni turned to each other as if to say, *what's he talking about?*

Danny saw it. "Look," he said, pointing to the pamphlet Newman had given the three boys after their summer tour. "Didn't either of you look it over? Freshmen and Sophomores have forty-five minutes for lunch. Say we amount to half the student body. That means about 750 of us have to eat and eat quick. So enjoy looking around now, because when school starts for real, this place will be a zoo."

The sudden push from behind caused Andrews to lurch forward, spitting out the last of his lunch.

"You're in my territory now, wetback. Your protector isn't going to do you any good here."

Andrews turned around to see Garrett Collison standing there with two of his friends. They were all smiling. The look on Danny Archer's face was anything but a smile. His eyes quickly zeroed in on Collison and then his two friends. *The taunt from Collison was just like before*, Danny thought, *full of confidence, even overconfidence.*

"And I'm not finished with you either, Archer," Collison added.

"Gentlemen, let's move it along, please," said one of the seniors who was serving as a lunch monitor.

Collison and his pals headed toward the conveyor belt to drop off their trays.

"That's not the way I wanted to start here," sighed Andrews.

151

Danny said nothing. He watched a sense of fear overtake his friend.

****

Chapter 16

"Well stranger, I wondered when I'd see you again," Newman said, as he attached his leash line to his ankle.

"I know," Danny answered. "Between school and my part time job at the market, I've been really busy."

"Then let's go," Newman said.

He and Danny paddled out through the waves. They spent the next hour or so trading off waves, occasionally taking the same wave, trying to see who could ride the longest.

"I love this," sighed Danny.

"You'll come to love a lot of things, young man. So, how do you like Burke?" Newman asked, as he turned to check out the next set.

"It's not bad," Danny replied. "In some ways, it's easier than I thought and in other ways, it's harder."

"Explain," replied Newman.

"Well, the paperwork isn't that hard. I mean the written assignments are really kind of easy."

"So what's the hard part?" Newman pressed.

"Having to talk," Danny said. "It's like on our tour when Mr. Wyckoff said we sit in a circle not in rows, so there can be discussion."

Newman nodded "yes".

"Well, I listen to what the teacher says and then I watch the group and listen to what someone will say. You know, Newman, like watching the waves and deciding which one you're going to take. Just when I think I have something to say, I think what I have to say isn't very important, so I keep quiet."

Newman turned to Danny and said, "Take the next one, Danny."

Danny paddled hard and caught the wave at just the right point. He was grinning when he got back to Newman.

"Wow, that was great. At first I thought it was a mistake to take it," Danny's face beamed with satisfaction.

"Danny, the real mistake would be to not take the wave because you think you're only going to get a little ride. If you don't talk in your class because you don't think you have much to say, you're making a mistake. When you and I are out here, don't we talk to each other about the waves?"

Danny nodded "yes".

"And when someone paddles back after a great ride or after getting dumped, you usually say 'great ride' or 'tough ride', right?"

"Yeah."

"It's no different at Burke or out here. Remember that."

****

"What's for dinner, Mom?" Danny called out from the backyard where he had stacked his surfboard against the fence and was preparing to take a shower.

"Bill is going to barbecue a tri-tip. He should be here soon," Debbie called out through the kitchen window.

After Danny changed into dry clothes, he grabbed a soda from the refrigerator.

"Bill seems to be coming over a lot lately," Danny said. He turned away so his mother would not see the impish grin forming on his face.

The pit of her stomach started to harden. Her throat constricted. She laid her towel on the sink.

"Danny, we need to talk."

He somehow managed to put on a somber face as he sat down at the table. She took his hands in hers.

"Danny, I'm never going to forget your father. He will always be a part of my memories, but..."

Danny looked at his mom. "But you want to have memories with Bill, right?"

Her neck muscles were practically paralyzed. She could barely nod "yes," much less say anything.

"Mom, I'm never going to forget Dad either, and I think both of us should start making memories with Bill."

****

As Bill pulled the tri-tip from the marinade bag, he felt something was different between him and Debbie and Danny. Not a bad something, but something he couldn't put his finger on.

"So, settling in at Burke?" He asked Danny, who had brought out sodas for each of them.

"So far, so good," Danny answered. "But there is one thing."

"What's that?" Bill asked, as he basted the tri-tip.

"Remember that Collison kid at Holy Cross I had a fight with?"

"How could I forget, Garrett Collison," Bill said.

He took a chair next to Danny. "Is he causing you trouble?"

"No, not yet," Danny said. "I think he's waiting for his chance, though."

"Afraid?" Bill asked.

"Of him, no way," Danny asserted, his chest puffing out slightly. "But he's started badmouthing one of my friends, Beni Andrews, at school. Beni told me his mom told him to walk away or run away from trouble."

"Sounds like good advice to me," Bill said.

Danny turned to Bill. "But what happens when trouble walks faster than you do or runs faster than you do? They've got a pretty strict code of conduct about fighting at school, you know."

This is sounding like a father-son talk, Bill thought. He chose his words carefully.

"There's no justification for starting a fight with Garrett Collison or anyone else. However, if you're trying to protect someone from being hurt by fighting off his attacker, in my mind, that's a different story. The only way a bully wins is when no one stands up to him."

****

157

There were four sections of freshmen at Burke Preparatory. Danny and his friend, Fletcher Williams, were lucky to be in the same section. Unfortunately for Beni Andrews, he was in the same section as Garrett Collison and a couple of his friends. Beni had several classes with them. Danny noticed in the ensuing weeks, Beni was bringing his lunch to school and not eating in the cafeteria. Instead, he chose to eat outside in the quad. Danny began bringing his lunch so he and Beni could spend time together.

"Why aren't you eating in the hall anymore?" Danny asked one day.

"No reason. I like it outside better," Andrews replied, his eyes avoiding making contact with Danny.

"Garrett Collison have anything to do with it?" Danny asked

Andrew stared at the ground, shaking his head "no". Danny didn't believe him for a second. In a minute, Archer had his proof. Garrett Collison and his two best friends, Andrew Koepp and William Sylvester, walked up to Archer and Andrews.

"That's right, the wetback eats outside on the grass," Collison sneered.

"Are you the wetback's friend, or should I say, amigo?" chimed in Koepp, while Sylvester laughed.

His temper was beginning to rise. Danny thought about his conversation with Newman and Bill.

"Yeah, I'm his friend. So what?" Danny snapped back.

Collison was feeling really brave with Tweedle Dumb and Tweedle Dee at his side.

"Well I'm not finished with him or you either, asshole!"

Archer leaned back, his elbows resting on the grassy knoll. He knew how to play this game.

"Yeah, well I heard that before too," Danny said. "I'm shaking in my shoes."

Danny saw Collison's fists clench. *Good, I got to him. Maybe just a little more.*

"Feel like a frog, Garrett?" A smile formed on Danny's face.

Collison's body started to move forward, but then he stopped.

"Let's go," he said to Koepp and Sylvester.

As they walked away, Collison subtly flashed his middle finger toward Danny and Andrews.

****

By Friday at lunchtime, Danny knew he would have to do more to protect his friend. When Danny joined Beni for lunch on the lawn that day, he saw Beni had a torn shirt pocket, several dirt smudges and a tear on his khaki pants.

"Beni, what happened?" Archer asked.

"It's nothing, really Danny, just let it go," Beni said.

"No, I won't let it go, Beni. It was Collison, wasn't it?"

"Please Danny, don't do anything. It will only get worse."

****

Danny stuck his head through the open door.

"Can I come in, Mr. Wyckoff?"

"Why sure, Danny. You're always welcome. How is Newman?"

"He's fine."

"Well, what can I do for you?"

"Mr. Wyckoff, my friend, Beni Andrews, is having a hard time with some of his classes and I thought if my friend, Fletcher Williams, and I could transfer into his section, maybe we could help. He could really use the help, Mr. Wyckoff," Danny pleaded.

"That's very kind of you and your friend. Let me see what I can do, Danny," Wyckoff said.

"Thank you, Mr. Wyckoff."

160

****

"Liz, do you think I could get off a little early today? My boyfriend is coming by to take me to the beach."

Diane Cano was a 16-year-old girl, half Filipino-half white, with the most beautiful cream complexion you could imagine, and endowed more than a girl of her age should be, according to Liz, owner of the Pleasure Point market.

"Danny, can you stay a little longer to cover for her?" Liz asked.

"No problem," Danny said.

Danny couldn't help but notice the disapproving frown on Liz's face.

"What's wrong, Liz?" He asked.

"That boyfriend of hers is a no good libidinous jerk. All he wants from Diane is..." She caught herself before she said anything more.

Danny walked to the front of the market in time to see Diane kiss Garrett Collison's older brother Dalton, and then climb into his Corvette.

****

"We're like the three musketeers again!" grinned Fletcher Williams, as he, Danny and Beni Andrews took their seats in Mr. Olson's American history class. Olson went to shut the door to his classroom when three late arrivals pushed through the door.

"Late again, gentlemen!" Olson said, as Garrett Collison, Andrew Koepp and William Sylvester took their seats, completely ignoring the teacher's admonition. Karl Olson took his place among the circled chairs.

"Today, our discussion will focus on Edmund Burke. I hope you have taken the time to read the pamphlet that was given to you during freshman orientation? Who would like to start with some facts about Edmund Burke?"

Olson's eyes searched the room for who would answer first. Danny Archer was equally assessing who would go first. Finally, Olson said, "Mr. Collison, tell us something about Edmund Burke."

Collison straightened up from his slouched back position. He cleared his throat as if he was going to make some grand proclamation.

"The school is named after Edmund Burke."

His answer evoked chuckles from his two friends and a frown from the teacher. Archer saw his chance. His hand went up.

"Mr. Archer," Olson said.

"Edmund Burke was a 17th century philosopher who was born in Dublin, Ireland."

"Very good, Mr. Archer," replied Olson.

"Mr. Koepp, would you like to explain Edmund Burke's thoughts about the American Revolution?"

It was soon apparent neither Collison, Koepp, or Sylvester had read the pamphlet handed out at freshman orientation.

"He supported the English," Koepp pronounced, while hiding his anxiety over his guess of an answer.

"Really?" groaned Olson.

Again, Archer saw his chance. His hand went up.

"Mr. Archer."

"Actually, Edmund Burke supported the colonists and felt the English should repeal the tea tax."

"Well said, Mr. Archer," came Olson's response.

Danny glanced across at Collison and Koepp with a "who's next" challenge in his eyes. *Newman was so right. Watch and pick your wave and your moment,* Danny thought. And so it went for the next few weeks. In every class they had, Collison and his pals were never prepared, while Danny, Fletcher and even Beni Andrews were always prepared. They seemed to take particular delight in waiting for some careless, half thought-out answer from Collison and his friends, and then pounce on it with their own response that would show them up.

****

Chapter 17

"Really?" Wyckoff replied. "Thanks for your input, Mark."

Wyckoff set the phone on its cradle. Not one of Beni Andrews' teachers reported any difficulty on the boy's part with classwork. If anything, Beni Andrews was at or near the top in all his classes. *Why the ruse from Danny Archer?* Wyckoff thought.

Calling for a meeting of the Freshman Advisory Council would have raised more attention than Wyckoff wanted. However, randomly talking with some members of the Freshman Advisory Council put no one under the spotlight. It didn't take Wyckoff long to find out that what he had suspected was true. If the freshmen Wyckoff talked to hadn't actually witnessed it, they heard about it. There had been instances of Hispanic students being called "wet backs", black students being taunted with "go back to the cotton fields", and in some cases, actual physical force being used. It was the same three names Wyckoff heard every time – Garrett Collison, Andrew Koepp and William Sylvester.

****

"Did you finish it?" Beni asked, as he, Danny and Fletcher headed up the stairs to the second floor for their math class.

"Yeah, it wasn't hard, Beni," Danny said. Looking up, he saw Collison and his pals at the head of the stairwell. As they started down, every student was subjected to an elbow or a trip. Beni headed up the right side of the stairwell. Danny and Fletcher were right behind him. Like a rogue wave, it wasn't hard to see what was coming. Danny was ready. Just as Collison passed Beni coming up the stairs, he threw his left elbow out to jab Andrews, and extended his left leg to trip him. At the last second, Danny grabbed Andrews and pushed him to the right against the wall. The force of Collison's elbow jab into the air momentarily caused him to lose his balance. Just for a second, Danny's extended left leg caught Collison's leg before he could right himself. To those who had been victims of Collison's abuse, it was a sight to see him flailing to keep his balance as Collison fell into those ahead of him. They grabbed the handrail to support themselves while Collison did a header down the stairs to the landing. In the chaos, those trying to get out of the way trampled over Collison's books, now scattered down the stairs.

By the time the hall monitor got to the scene, the snickers had erupted into outright laughter.

"What happened?" Mr. Greene asked. The answers came fast and furious.

"Oh, Collison was rushing down the stairs and tripped. "He lost his balance, Mr. Greene." "You shouldn't take the stairs two at a time," said another.

166

Collison was more embarrassed than hurt. "Get out of my way," he hollered, as he bent over to pick up his books. "Here, this one must be yours," said Beni Andrews, who made no attempt to hide the smile on his face.

****

If his fall hadn't been bad enough, the whispered comments like "Hey, twinkle toes" or "Hey, stumble bum" were driving Collison crazy. Like any bully, he turned his attention not to the one he knew had tripped him, but to the weakest one.

"Where's the wetback hang out?" Collison asked, as he and Koepp watched Andrews and Archer headed down the street after school.

"I hear he likes to hang out at Pleasure Point," Koepp replied.

"Good, I'll meet you and Sylvester at the market Sunday about noon," Collison said.

****

The red Corvette had been idling outside of her market so long, Liz finally went to the window to see when her helper was coming in. His right arm was around her shoulder, pulling her closer to him. She wasn't resisting until his left hand started sliding up her leg.

"I said no, Dalton!" she said, forcefully pushing his hand away.

Diane Cano was already regretting last night when she had allowed Dalton to go farther than she wanted. Unfortunately, she had lit the fuse and it wouldn't take long for it to go off.

"What's the big deal? It's only sex," he groused.

"Not to me," she snapped. "It's about caring for me."

She got out of the car and slammed the door. She paused long enough to straighten out her blouse and hopefully get an apology. Dalton got out of the car and walked around to her.

"You know I care about you. I'm sorry. I really am," he said.

Cano was angry at him and angrier at herself for caring. She allowed him to give her a hug.

"When do you work again?" he whispered.

"Monday night, five to nine," she answered.

"See you then, Babe."

When Dalton pulled away, she came across the street to the market.

"He's no good, you know," Liz said when Diane came into the market.

"Oh, he's not that bad, Liz," Cano said apologetically.

Liz looked at the young 16-year-old she had come to think of as her own.

"Sweetie, don't settle for 'not so bad'."

****

"That should do it, Jack," Newman said, as he finished attaching the last wire nut. "You can rest a little easier," he added.

Jack O'Neil's house sat on the cliffs where 36th Ave. intersected with East Cliff Drive. Hopefully this project would give him a little more security from passersby.

"Newman, I really appreciate it," O'Neil said. "Say, are you surfing today?"

"Yeah, I thought I'd give 'The Lane' a try," Newman answered.

"Not Pleasure Point?" O'Neill asked.

"No. You know, Jack, every so often Pleasure Point is a little too tame for me."

"Know what you mean, buddy," replied O'Neil.

If Newman only knew, Pleasure Point would be anything but tame that afternoon.

****

Beni Andrews was waiting for Danny at the bottom of the stairs where 36th Ave. meets East Cliff Drive. He envied Danny's ability to surf, or more correctly, to not be afraid of the ocean. He climbed the rock pile to get a better vantage point.

"Hey, Beni," Danny called out from the handrail.

Beni waved back. Danny lifted up his surf board and headed down the stairs. About 50 yards away toward the market, the three of them stood watching.

"See him?" asked Collison.

"Yeah," replied Koepp. "The beaner is there too, sitting on the rocks."

Most of the late afternoon surfers were farther down past Jack O'Neil's house at "The Hook". There was only one couple watching from the handrail on the cliffs.

"Sure you don't want to come out, just a little way?" Danny asked. Beni smiled. "Not yet."

Danny attached his leash line and paddled out to the whitewater. He had just turned his board toward shore when he noticed Beni backing up on the rock pile. Three other kids stood at the bottom. Danny recognized Collison, Koepp and Sylvester. When the three jumped up on the rocks and pulled Beni down to the sand, Danny paddled like hell toward shore. He kept his eyes on them. When they started hitting and

170

kicking Beni, Danny paddled so hard he thought his shoulders would fall off.

Once he was in shallow water and close enough, he shouted, "Get off of him!"

By now Andrews was curled up in a fetal position trying to protect himself.

"Go get him, I'll take care of the 'spic'," Collison said.

Danny was on shore when Koepp and Sylvester came charging toward him. They may have thought it was two on one, but Danny had a surf board. The challenge came, "You're gonna get yours, Archer."

At that moment, Danny shifted his surf board chest high and threw it at the two aggressors. Koepp's right arm took the brunt of the force. The twin skaggs of the board raked across Sylvester's thigh, as a thin trickle of blood appeared. Koepp was screaming as he cradled what was probably a broken arm to his chest. Sylvester wanted no more of Archer. Danny ran toward his friend Beni.

"Now I'll finish what I started," Collison yelled.

The sight of Andrews lying in the sand with a bloody nose and a lower lip split wide open incensed Danny. He charged Collison. Collison took a bladed karate type stance, and attempted a leg swipe. The shifting sand caused his leg to go too high. Danny stepped into it, his right arm grabbing Collison's leg at the knee. Danny jerked Collison forward and slammed his fist into Collison's face. Collison's right leg crumpled and he fell to the ground. Danny was on him like some kind of wild animal. His fists flailed away, ignoring Collison's pleas that he'd had enough. Danny only stopped because he was out of breath. When he finally stood up, Andrews said, "Danny, we need to get out of here."

Catching his breath, Danny stepped over Collison.

"Come on, we'll go to my house."

A couple had come down the stairs after hearing all the commotion. Collison yelled to them, "He attacked us first. It was him," he said, pointing to Archer and Andrews, who were now at the top of the stairs.

****

"My God! not him again, Danny." Debbie Archer sank into the couch when Danny told her of his encounter with Collison and his friends.

"Mom, I couldn't just run away. They had Beni surrounded on the ground, kicking him. I hollered for them to stop, but they wouldn't. What was I supposed to do?"

His voice had equal amounts of frustration and fear in it.

"I know. I know, Danny," she said.

She pulled the boy to her and hugged him as tight as she ever had. Debbie turned her attention to Beni, who had a cold compress pressed against his lower lip.

"How is it?" she asked.

"It stings a little," came the muted response.

"Let me see," Debbie said, gently taking hold of the towel.

Andrews' lower lip was puffed up, making it look worse than it really was. His nose seemed slightly swollen and there were some abrasions on his back and legs where he had been kicked.

"I think I'd better call your mom, Beni," Debbie said.

The boy nodded "okay" as he put the compress back on his lip.

****

"That's everything?" Evans asked. He had been on patrol when dispatch contacted him to call a Debbie Archer, ASAP. "You can count on one thing, Danny. This will be just like the first time. You'll be the one who started everything."

Debbie weighed in, "That's what I'm afraid of, Bill."

"Then let's get ready," he said. "Danny, Beni, I want you two to write down everything that happened.

You know who did what, who said what. I'll do some checking to see if any complaints against Danny have been filed by Garrett's family."

****

The ride to school Monday was particularly quiet. Beni Andrews' mother had decided to keep him home for a few days. Fletcher Williams sat spellbound after hearing his friend's account of what had happened. As for Danny Archer, a strange thing had happened. He was still angry. Not so much at Collison and his pals. They were jerks as far as Danny was concerned. No, he was angry as to why it had happened at all. Why should someone be picked on because of the color of their skin or what country his parents came from or where they attended church? The more he thought about it, the angrier he became.

"You know the word's out?" Williams said, as they got off the bus.

"I'll bet," Archer said, as he slung his backpack over his shoulder.

He seemed to stand a little taller, Williams thought, *and with a bit more confidence as well.*

With Collison, Koepp, and Sylvester missing from school, rumors abounded. Some believed that Garrett Collison was in the hospital near death from a brutal attack at the hands of Danny Archer. Andrew Koepp could lose his leg and William Sylvester had broken ribs and a punctured lung after Archer attacked him with his surfboard. Others thought they were just three rich punks who picked on the wrong kid.

"Man, I can't tell if you're the heavyweight champion of the world or if you've got leprosy," Williams said, as they walked the length of the second floor to get to their history class.

"It doesn't really matter," answered Danny, who was now thinking about something Newman and Evans had once said to him – consequences.

****

"I checked. Nothing's been filed with the PD," Bill said.

His words did little to alleviate the fear Debbie Archer felt in the pit of her stomach as she prepared dinner.

"So, no news is good news?" Debbie said, her hands nervously shredding lettuce into a salad bowl.

"At this point, yes," Evans replied.

"Damn," Debbie muttered after checking the refrigerator for milk. "Danny, can you ride to the market and get a quart of milk? I need it to make the salad dressing."

Evans handed the boy a couple of bucks. "Keep the change," he said with a grin.

"Oh, that will make me rich," came the comic retort.

Chapter 18

Danny rode down 36th Avenue to East Cliff Drive, then turned right toward the market. This way he got a glimpse of the ocean. When he got to the crosswalk at 32nd Ave., he saw the red Corvette parked in front of the market. He recognized it right away as belonging to Garrett Collison's older brother, Dalton. Danny leaned his bike against the newspaper rack. As he headed into the market, he glanced inside the Corvette. Three empty plastic circles indicated the driver was drinking. Danny headed to the dairy section. When he opened the door, he heard her.

"Danny!"

Diane Cano had called out his name to stop her boyfriend's unwanted advances. Dalton turned toward him.

"You're the little prick that beat up my brother yesterday," came the accusation.

Danny said nothing. He grabbed a quart of milk and headed to the counter. Cano was waiting for him. She took his money and gave him the change. Danny headed to the door.

"Not so brave now, you little asshole," Dalton gloated, his bravery soaring after downing half a six-pack.

Dalton Collison's Napoleonic size was not the reason Danny did not respond. He stopped halfway to the door. It was either get in a fight or walk away. This time he listened to the little voice in his head. Without turning around, he said, "I don't want any trouble," and continued to the door.

He heard the first yell when he got to his bike. A car loaded with kids passed by at that moment. *Must be them*, Danny thought. He got to the crosswalks when he heard it again. This time it wasn't a yell. It was more like a scream and it didn't come from any passing car. It came from inside the market.

The little voice didn't say a thing. It didn't have to. Danny Archer knew what he was going to do. He followed the sounds of Diane Cano's cries. He found her behind the counter, lying on the floor. Dalton Collison was on his knees, straddling her. The force of his slap startled Danny.

"You bitch! What the hell did you think I was after?" Collison screamed.

With all his might, Danny threw his backpack at Collison. The force knocked Collison off the girl and onto his side.

"You son-of-a-bitch!" he cursed, as he struggled to his feet while trying to pull up his pants. "I'm going to beat your ass," he roared.

Cano saw her chance. She hurried to her feet and headed toward the back door. Danny ran to the front door. When Collison got around the corner, he saw Archer was gone.

"I'm going to get you," Collison roared, as he headed toward the front door.

Danny controlled his breathing. For an instant, he let his body relax. He focused his mind. He stood next to the wall outside the door, his hands clenching tight around the back of a metal chair he had grabbed from a nearby table. When Dalton appeared in the doorway, Danny swung the chair at Dalton's knees. The pain was unbearable, as Collison collapsed on the ground, sputtering unintelligible cries of both revenge and pleas for help. Danny grabbed his bike and rode home faster than he ever had before.

****

After listening to Danny's story, Evans immediately drove to the market. No Corvette was in front. There were two patrol officers talking to a woman who lived in a house across the street from the market. Evans approached them.

"What brings you here, Bill?" Officer Smith asked.

"I was just listening to my police scanner when I heard the call come in. I don't live too far from here, so I thought I'd stop by to see if I could help. Were you able to get the information from this lady?"

Smith took Evans out of earshot of the woman.

"Not much, Bill," Smith said. "She heard some screaming from inside the market. Apparently she likes to keep her windows open. She saw a young kid lurking at the front door. When another boy appeared to be coming out of the market, she said the one hiding outside swung a chair at the other boy's legs."

"Was she able to identify either one of the boys?" Evans asked.

"She recognized the boy who swung the chair as someone she has seen at the market before. She thinks he might work there."

"Well, I'll get out of your way. It looks like you've got everything under control."

****

When Evans got to Danny's home, he found Debbie cradling her son in her arms. Danny Archer was a 13-year-old scrapper who wasn't afraid to fight, if necessary. He had grown to respect the ocean and the waves it produced, but he wasn't afraid of either. Nothing Kelly Raye had taught him about controlling anxiety and fear was helping him now. Things were different. Nothing anyone had ever said to him seemed to help. Everything was spinning out of control.

There was one person who knew exactly what Danny was going through. Someone who at a young age had his life ripped apart, leaving him with no hope and no chance for the future. He would not disappoint the boy.

****

Over the next few days, it seemed nothing went right for Danny Archer. For one, Diane Cano was nowhere to be found, so the police had no way to verify Archer's story. In addition to looking through the store, one of the officers found a butcher knife on the floor near the front door. It seemed to bolster Garrett Collison's claim that Danny had threatened him after he, Collison, had stopped Archer from harassing Diane Cano.

Though uninvited, Newman was a welcome addition to the strategy meeting Fred Wyckoff had Debbie Archer arrange at her house.

"Just so everybody understands, there are two independent processes taking place simultaneously. One is the police investigation. Bill can address that issue. The other is a demand by Wilson Collison for the Faculty/Student Committee on Conduct to review the circumstances of the attacks on his sons, Garrett and Dalton. Wilson is adamant he'll settle for nothing less than immediate expulsion of Danny."

"But I didn't attack anyone," Danny exclaimed, an emotion of frustration all too apparent in his voice.

"I believe you, Danny. Everyone here believes you. The issue with the attack on Garrett is his father has statements from two people who said they saw you straddling Garrett beating him with your fist."

"But they didn't see what led up to that!" Debbie shouted, her frustration equaling that of her son.

"Until we find someone who did, we have a pretty tall mountain to climb," Wyckoff stated.

"One question," Newman asked. "When is this meeting of that faculty committee you spoke of?"

"I managed to put it off until this Friday at 3 PM. That gives us a little over three days to come up with something," Wyckoff said.

"That's not much time," Debbie said.

"It's all the time we've got," Evans added. "The PD has contacted Diane Cano's family and friends. The family is stonewalling the investigation and none of her friends have heard from her. The police department has received a complaint from the Collison family's attorney. You can expect them to ask that Danny be charged with assault and battery."

"Who speaks at this meeting Friday?" Newman asked.

"Wilson's attorney, Ashton Collins, will argue their side. Anyone from Danny's family can speak on his behalf," answered Wyckoff.

Newman stood up. "Danny, Debbie, Bill, I'd like to be that person who speaks on Danny's behalf. I'll be gone for a few days, but I promise I'll be back in time. I wouldn't ask if it weren't really important to me."

Debbie and Bill looked at each other.

"I trust him, Mom," Danny said.

Smiles formed on Debbie's and Bill's faces.

"We trust him too," Evans said. "It's yours, Newman."

****

It was the first time Bill Evans spent the night at Debbie's house. She needed him to stay and Danny wanted him to stay. If ever the deck had been stacked against someone, it was stacked against Danny now. Money and influence were formidable opponents of the truth. Evans adjusted Danny's tie.

"I want you to know, regardless of how this turns out, I understand why you did what you did and I'm proud of you."

Danny looked at Evans, "But the consequences Bill, what about the consequences?"

Evans sat down on his bed.

"Son, when you have to decide what's the right thing to do and you let the possible consequences just determine what you do, you'll wind up doing something less than the right thing. You know what Newman once told me about consequences?"

Danny stood up and stared into the mirror on the wall. "Once you decide a wave is the right one to take, take it. If you worry about wiping out, you don't belong on a surfboard."

Evans stood up next to Danny and stared into the mirror. "Let's do this."

****

The hearing was scheduled for the President's conference room. Wilson Collison's attorney, along with Wilson and his two sons, were already seated when Danny, his mom, and Bill Evans arrived.

"Mrs. Archer, Officer Evans, Danny, please take your place at the table to your left," Fred Wyckoff said.

The setup reminded Evans of some sort of congressional hearing. On a small raised platform five faculty members and four senior students sat behind a long table. Wyckoff looked at his watch.

"Who will be speaking on behalf of Garrett and Dalton Collison?" Wyckoff asked.

The $500 suit stood up. "Ashton Collins, senior legal counsel for Wilson Collison."

Wyckoff looked at the Archers.

"And for Daniel Archer?"

Debbie and Evans both looked over their shoulders.

"Mr. Newman," Debbie answered. The uncertainty in her voice brought a smile to the attorney for the Collison family.

Wyckoff knew he could only stall for so long.

"So everyone understands how this proceeding works, the committee will hear the allegations of Code of Conduct violations as alleged by the Collison family. We will then listen to any statements from the Archer family. The committee will then retire to determine if a violation of the Code of Conduct has occurred, and any possible consequences."

Just then the doors to the conference room opened. The gentleman with shoulder length black hair with streaks of grey entered the room.

"My apologies, Fred. Newman asked me to say he's running a little late, but he will be here soon."

"For the benefit of the committee members and the Wilson family, this is Jack O'Neil. I presume you are here for the Archer family?" Wyckoff asked.

"Yes," O'Neill said, taking a chair behind the Archer family.

"I'll give Mr. Newman a few more minutes," Wyckoff said, much to the consternation of Collins.

It couldn't have been five minutes before the door opened again and Newman entered, pushing a cart with the TV set on it.

"My apologies to everyone," Newman said.

"Can we finally begin?" Collison's attorney asked.

"Please begin, Mr. Collins," Wyckoff said

Newman gathered the Archers together. He whispered, "No matter what he says, don't react. He'll try to bait you for a reaction. Don't give him the satisfaction."

Ashton Collins was as methodical as an attorney arguing a capital murder case. He started with the Garrett Collison issue. He presented copies of the reports of Collison, Koepp, and Sylvester. Then he added the reports of the couple who came upon the attack. If that wasn't enough, he had reports from the emergency room physician who tended to the boys. To hear Collins interpretation, the unprovoked attack by Danny Archer left the three boys on death's doorstep. Lastly, he gave the committee copies of Garrett and Dalton's report from the first assault when Garrett was at Holy Cross Elementary School.

The final insult was Collins' admonition to ignore any report from Officer Evans which had been submitted, as Officer Evans was involved in a sexual relationship with the boy's mother at the time. It was all Evans could do to stay in his chair. Debbie Archer was not so controlled. She jumped to her feet and yelled, "That's a lie!"

Newman was able to calm her down and settle her back into her chair.

"Anything more regarding Garrett Collison?" Wyckoff asked.

"No, I'll proceed with the attack on Dalton Collison," Collins said.

What a scumbag!, Evans thought. According to the Collison's family attorney, it was Dalton who pushed Danny away from Diane Cano when Dalton arrived at the market and found Danny Archer harassing her. It was Danny Archer who had grabbed the butcher knife and threatened to kill Dalton. And it was Archer who stood next to the entrance waiting to attack Dalton when he pursued Archer. Lastly, the report was read from the little old lady who lived across the street from the market. Finally, it was over.

"Mr. Newman, your turn," Wyckoff said.

Newman stood up. "Before I begin my presentation, I would ask that the committee members keep in mind a quote attributed to Edmund Burke: 'The only thing necessary for evil to triumph is for good men to do nothing'."

Newman pushed the cart with the TV set forward so it could be seen by everyone.

"Jack, can you give me the tape, please?"

O'Neill came forward and handed Newman a VHS cassette.

"Members of the committee, Mr. O'Neill will attest to the fact that this is a VHS cassette from his home security system. His home is on the cliff side of

East Cliff Drive, overlooking the location of the alleged attack. When you watch it, note the date/time stamp in the upper left-hand corner. It is the same date and time Mr. Collins alleges Garrett Collison was attacked by Daniel Archer."

Newman pressed play and sat down. Every person in the room was glued to the screen except for Ashton Collins. His head bobbled back and forth from the TV screen to Wilson Collison with a look that said, *"You've got to be shitting me! Where did this come from and why didn't I know about it?"*

The committee saw Garrett, Koepp and Sylvester drag Beni Andrews off the rocks and begin hitting and kicking him. The camera caught Koepp and Sylvester charging toward Danny as he got to shore. They were yelling and had their fists clenched. The throwing of the surfboard looked like just what it was – self-defense. There were several groans when they saw Garrett Collison repeatedly kick a defenseless Andrews who was laying on the sand. From Newman's perspective, some on the committee looked as though they wanted to stand up and cheer when Danny Archer pulled Collison off of Beni Andrews and gave Collison a dose of his own medicine. When the tape ended, Newman pressed eject and handed the tape back to O'Neill.

"That's all regarding the Garrett Collison issue," Newman said, unashamedly mocking the Collison's attorney.

Fred Wyckoff had a sudden new fondness for Newman.

"As for the Dalton Collison issue? Wyckoff asked.

"One moment," Newman said. He walked to the door of the conference room and into the hallway. He returned with two Santa Cruz Police Department officers and a young teenage girl – Diane Cano.

"Members of the committee, this is Diane Cano. In her culture, a girl who has been raped is viewed as unworthy to be given in marriage by her family. She was staying with family members in San Francisco to avoid the shame she felt she brought upon her family. I convinced her to come back and talk to the police. Here is a copy of her statement, where she describes in detail the sexual assault by Dalton Collison, exactly as detailed in Daniel Archer's statement, including the part where Dalton Collison grabbed a butcher knife from the sandwich table and chased after Daniel Archer, threatening to kill him."

Newman walked back to the two officers and took an envelope from each one. He returned to the table.

Holding up one envelope he said, "This is a copy of Ms. Cano's statement. I have prepared copies for each of the committee members as well as the Collison family."

Holding up a second envelope, Newman said, "And this is a warrant for the arrest of Dalton Collison on sexual assault charges filed by Diane Cano. At the conclusion of this hearing, these two police officers will take Dalton Collison into custody."

Newman sat down. He smiled when he saw how the committee looked at the Collison family.

****

Chapter 19

"How long do you think it will take them?" Debbie asked.

"After Newman's presentation, I don't imagine very long," Evans said.

The late afternoon fog brought a chill to the air outside the administration building where the Archers stood. The first to appear were the two police officers with Dalton Collison in cuffs. They were followed by the Collison's family attorney, who was anxiously assuring Dalton and his family everything was under control. Lastly, Newman appeared with Diane Cano.

"I owe you a lot, young lady," Newman said.

"No, I owe you a lot and I owe Danny even more," she said.

Newman turned toward Danny.

"Be ready for school Monday," he said. "And don't worry about Garrett and his friends. All three will be looking for new schools."

"Are you sure, Newman?" Danny asked, not believing what he had heard.

"Trust me," Newman said. "Take the wave."

****

"Did you ever think this day would come?" Fletcher Williams asked his best friend.

"I had my doubts," Danny Archer answered, "especially with that hearing with the Faculty/Student Conduct Committee in our freshman year."

"How do I look?" Beni Andrews interrupted, as he slowly turned in his graduation cap and gown.

"Just like the rest of us, only brown," joked Williams.

"Yeah, yeah," Andrews smirked.

Fred Wyckoff, adorned in his robes signifying he had a Ph.D., gave the graduates-to-be a last word of advice.

"Ladies and gentlemen. I will not have a chance to address you again as a group, so please afford me this opportunity to do so. I am immensely proud of each and every one of you. For some of you, this day marks the fulfillment of expectations from generations of Burke graduates in your family. For others, the only expectation you had was to get through the next test."

Fletcher Williams could not contain his comical self, as he shouted, "That would be me, Mr. Wyckoff."

"Yes, Fletcher, I know. Remember, I was your freshman English teacher."

The little repartee took some of the nervous edge off everyone.

"For all of you, from your first day at Burke, you wondered what to expect from someone who was different from you, someone whose skin color was different, someone who came from a family of greater or lesser affluence than yours, or someone whose native tongue was not English. If you have learned anything from attending Burke, I hope it is this; value a person by the compassion in their heart and the fairness of their ideas."

The 350 or so graduates began to shuffle in line at the sound of "Pomp and Circumstance." They entered the auditorium single file down both sides of the Hall. Every parent's eyes were on one person, their son or daughter. The only ones paying attention to the valedictorian's speech were his family. The call for diplomas was what everyone was waiting for. At last it came and with it, Sandra Acton's family violated the president's request to hold the applause until all graduates had received their diplomas.

At day's end, Newman and Danny sat high upon the rocks, looking out to the sea. Danny looked like he had lost his pet dog. Newman knew what a wonderful, adventurous future Danny had in front of him. Newman also knew what it was like to have no future at all.

"Enough with the long face, Danny," Newman said. "You're headed to Berkeley, Beni got a full ride to Stanford and Fletcher's going to St. Mary's College in Moraga. The three of you are less than an hour and a half from each other and two hours from here. Could it get any better?"

Danny looked up to see a smiling Newman.

"You always seem to say the right thing at the right time," Danny replied.

"I've said enough of the wrong thing to ultimately be right once in awhile," Newman replied. "Are you considering a major, or are you going to wing it for a year or two?"

"No, I pretty much made up my mind to major in Criminology and be a cop like Bill," Danny said

"I didn't see that one coming," mused Newman.

"Really?" Danny asked. "After all, you are the reason I picked it."

"Now I am baffled," grinned Newman.

"Come on Newman. Remember what you said at the Faculty/Student Conduct Committee hearing in my freshman year?"

"Not really," lied Newman.

"You told them to consider a quote attributed to Edmund Burke: "The only thing necessary for evil to triumph is for good men to do nothing.""

Newman was feeling pretty good about himself and about Danny

****

The next few years passed too fast. Danny not only got his BA in Criminology at Cal, he finished his Master's degree as well. Beni Andrews got a Bachelor of Science in Structural Engineering and landed a six figure job with Bechtel Corporation. As for Fletcher Williams, he parlayed a degree in English Literature, and a teaching credential from St. Mary's College, into teaching freshman English at none other than Burke Preparatory.

****

Newman was thrilled when he got his invitation to Danny Archer's graduation from the police academy. He wouldn't have missed it for the world, in spite of the persistent cough he hadn't been able to shake for the last few months.

"Glad you could make it, Newman," Bill Evans said. "Maybe you could sit with Debbie. I have to be up on the stage."

"It would be my pleasure to sit with the beautiful Mrs. Evans," Newman said, giving Bill and Debbie a full swashbuckling bow at the waist.

Debbie smiled, as she moved to make room for Newman.

"You must be pretty proud of him," Newman asked.

"I certainly am," Debbie said, as she gently rolled the two carat wedding ring on her finger. "He's worked so hard to get where he is today."

"I was referring to Danny," Newman said.

Realizing her faux pas, Debbie's embarrassed words stumbled out.

"Oh my God! Of course I'm proud of Danny as well. Bill's promotion and Danny's appointment to the PD all came in the same month, and it's been kind of overwhelming."

After a few remarks by the mayor, Bill Evans' old partner, now Lieutenant Hal Wilson, took the microphone.

"Chief William Evans will now present the graduates with their badges. Attention!" The dozen rookie officers snapped to their feet and rendered a hand salute to the recently appointed Chief of Police. The chief rendered one in kind.

"Our profession is often referred to as the thin blue line," Evans said, as he addressed the audience. "It is a very thin line indeed, for one person and one person only stands between a potential victim and the criminal. That person is your son or daughter who is standing here today. It is my great pleasure to present the gold shield to these who have chosen to serve and protect. Officer Daniel Archer, please step forward."

Danny took the three steps up to the podium. Chief Evans pinned the shield number 7524 on Danny's dress blue jacket.

"I can't tell you how proud I am of you, Son," he said.

"Thanks, Dad. I'm proud of you as well."

They shook hands, stepped back, and rendered each other a hand salute.

****

Chapter 20

One Year Later

"Honey, there is a letter here for you from some law firm here in Santa Cruz. What do you know about Spinella and Son?" Debbie asked her husband.

"Not much," Bill said. "I think they do estates and wills. What does it say?"

Debbie opened the envelope and read its contents.

"There is going to be some sort of estate settlement for someone named John Peralta. We've been asked to attend."

After the signatory of Anthony Spinella Junior, Debbie Archer saw a list of those who had been cc'ed; Father Mike from Holy Cross, Fred Wyckoff, and her son, Danny Archer.

When Debbie showed the letter to Bill, he said, "I need to make some calls."

When he was finished calling those cc'ed on the letter, he turned to his wife. "No one's ever heard of a John Peralta."

"Well, apparently he knows us and everyone else as well," Debbie replied.

Glancing back at the letter, Bill said "I guess we'll find out who this John Peralta is this Thursday."

****

The Law office of Anthony Spinella Junior was located in an old Victorian about a block from the Santa Cruz Hotel, which, in fact, was not a hotel, but a rather nice Italian restaurant. Bill and Debbie Archer had parked in a public parking lot across the street. They were standing at the corner waiting for a break in traffic to cross the street, when a voice called out, "Bill, wait for us." Fred Wyckoff and Father Mike hurried to catch them.

"Where's Danny?" Father Mike asked.

"He told me he'd meet us here," Bill said.

A courteous driver finally stopped and waited for them to pass. Father Mike waved a "thank you" to the driver who recognized the black clothes and white collar as those of a Catholic priest. He hollered, "Do I get a pass for this Sunday, Father?" He sped off without waiting for an answer.

****

"Mr. Spinella will be right with you. Please follow me to his conference room," his secretary said.

The 12-foot walls were richly decorated with mahogany panels and shelf after shelf filled with law books.

"There is cold water and iced tea, should you want some," the secretary said, pointing to a table near the window. Father Mike got an iced tea for Debbie and waters for himself and Bill. Debbie glanced at her watch impatiently, but before she could say anything, Danny was escorted into the conference room by the secretary.

"Parking is a bitch!" he said, then immediately offered an apology to Father Mike and his mother.

Danny had just taken a swig of water when Anthony Spinella entered the room, followed by a young woman whose attractiveness immediately caught Danny Archer's eye.

"I want to thank you for coming today. I'm sure you all have busy schedules so allow me to get started. First, let me introduce Angela Stevens. She is a nurse who works with Hospice."

That bit of news caused the group to look at each other. It was Debbie who spoke for all of them.

"Mr. Spinella, I don't believe any of us knows anyone under Hospice care."

Spinella took his glasses off and laid them on the table.

"There is no easy way to tell you this," he said. "You knew him as Newman. What you didn't know is that Newman had been under Hospice care for the last six months. He passed away last week. Angela was his caregiver during that time."

Fred Wyckoff slumped back in his chair and unashamedly said, "Shit!" Father Mike closed his eyes and made a sign of the cross. Bill Evans put his arms around his wife and pulled her close to him.

"Oh Bill! Newman was so special." Her words were barely audible between the flow of tears pouring down her face.

Danny slammed his fist on the table. "No, God dammit, no," he shouted. "Not Newman. He's always been there."

Danny quickly stood up and went to the window. He didn't want anyone to see his tears, but he cared for naught if they saw him wipe his eyes with his uniform sleeve.

The young nurse got up and walked over to Danny. She placed her hand on his shoulder.

"Everyone here was very special to Newman, but I think you were his favorite, Officer Archer. Not a day passed that he didn't talk about you."

Danny turned to the nurse, his eyes still damp.

"Why didn't he say anything? I mean about being sick," he asked.

"Newman was a very private man, Officer Archer. He asked me to say nothing whenever we saw one of you. Besides, he felt you all had plenty to worry about. Father Mike had his hands full at Holy Cross. Mr. Wyckoff with his charges at Burke didn't have a spare minute in his day to worry about him. Chief Evans' new promotion kept his plate full, and Danny, he felt you should have a chance to dream, not watch an old man die. Those were his words," she said.

For several uncomfortable minutes, everyone sat silent, seeking solace in their memories of Newman. It was Bill Evans who broke the ice.

"Mr. Spinella, I'm confused on a couple of points."

"How can I help?" The attorney replied.

"First, Stevens said something about Newman seeing us. How is that possible? The second question is why are we talking about Newman when your letter said something about the estate of a John Peralta?"

"I can answer the first question," the nurse said. "When Newman was diagnosed with stage IV lymphatic cancer a little over a year ago, Mr. O'Neill graciously allowed Newman to live in the lower level of his house. We used to watch whenever any of you came down to the beach to surf."

She looked at Danny. "He really enjoyed watching you. He used to say you the most natural surfer he had ever seen."

201

A smile formed on Danny's face.

"I'll address your second question, Mr. Evans," said the attorney. What Anthony Spinella told them sent them into a state of shock.

****

"You knew him as Newman. His real name was John Peralta. He was raised on a dairy farm outside of Hollister, California. John's father, Larry Peralta, was killed in the latter part of World War II. The operation of the dairy fell upon John and his mother. Up to his death, Larry and his wife made sure John spent a month or more with Larry's sister who lived here in Santa Cruz."

"That's when he developed his love for the ocean and surfing," Danny interrupted.

"Correct, Officer," replied Spinella. "In the summer of 1947, a second tragedy struck the Peralta family. Over the Fourth of July weekend that summer, several thousand motorcycle gangs took over the town of Hollister. The movie, "The Wild One", starring Marlon Brando was based on that weekend. There were drunken brawls all over town. Every business suffered some sort of property damage."

He continued. "Around noon on Monday, Sara Peralta left John at the dairy and went to town to pick up a few food items. She told John she would only be an hour or so. Living outside of town, they hadn't heard much of what was going on in Hollister. Three hours later when she hadn't returned, John took the family truck and drove to town to find his mother.

"This isn't going to turn out good, is it?" asked Bill Evans.

"In the short run no, it isn't," said Spinella. "When I'm done, then you can decide how things turned out."

Spinella went on to tell them how John went to the local market owned by Sam Luna. A half a dozen motorcycles were parked outside the store. Scores of empty beer cans littered the sidewalk. When John started to walk to the door, a drunken gang member warned John to stay outside. John ignored him.

When he got inside, the scene looked like an earthquake had struck the store. Display racks were strewn everywhere, broken liquor bottles were scattered about. Sam Luna, the owner, was on his knees at the end of the counter. A blood soaked towel covered his face. John ran to his side. He asked Sam what had happened and if he was okay. Terror spread throughout John's body, when Sam pulled a towel away from his face and through smashed lips and a jaw that jutted out at an angle, told John to get out of here before they came back. John pleaded for Sam to tell him if his mother had been there. Before he sagged to the floor unconscious, Sam managed to tell John the gang members had dragged his mother to Sam's office.

John ran to Sam's office where he found his mother lying on the floor. Her dress was practically ripped from her body. Her face was bruised. Blood flowed from her nose. John sank to his knees, cradling his mother in his arms.

Spinella looked at those around the table. "No boy should ever see his mother that way and it explains why John reacted the way he did."

Father Mike's hand held the rosary in his pocket as his fingers deftly passed over one bead and then another. Debbie Archer's hands were like a vice grip on her husband's arm as they listened to the rest of the story.

Before she passed out, Sara Peralta was able to give her son a description of the two men who had attacked her. It was more than anger that raged through John's body. It was a Satanic eruption. John grabbed a bag Sam kept in the office. He walked furtively down the aisle until he saw the two men his mother had described. One was buckling up his pants while the other hoisted a couple of cases of beer onto his shoulders. Neither one saw John coming. His first swing crushed the skull of the one buckling up his pants, who collapsed like a ragdoll. John's second swing caught the other one in the face. His nose and orbital socket shattered upward into his brain. He was dead before he hit the floor. That's when the gang member who had warned John not to go in came looking for his friends. John left him clutching broken ribs.

"Newman did all that?" Danny asked, as he remembered the day Newman dragged a surfer off his board.

"Yes, he did," Spinelli said. "He paid a horrible price for it. By Monday noon that day, hundreds of police from nearby cities were rounding up the remaining gang members. They came across the scene at Sam's market as John was carrying his mother to her car. The police gave John an escort to the local hospital.

In the months that followed, John Peralta went from a teenage hero who had avenged his mother's brutal rape to a vigilante madman. John's mother had a complete mental break. She couldn't corroborate any of John's story. Ultimately she was placed in a sanitarium and passed away three years later. The surviving gang member testified John attacked his two friends and himself without provocation. Fortunately for John, he had a good attorney, my father, William Spinella. Dad argued because of John's age and a somewhat supporting story from Sam Luna, that John should not sentenced to state prison but rather to a reform school at the California Boys Republic in Chino, California. The judge agreed and John was sentenced to Boys Republic for five years.

Debbie gasped when she heard the words "five years." The nurse saw the anguish on Danny Archer's face. She wanted to reach out to him, and she knew he needed time.

"Mr. Spinella, I don't see how any of this turns out good," sighed Debbie, whose eyes poured out an endless stream of tears.

There was a knock on the door and Spinella's secretary came in.

"He's here," she said.

"Good. Send him in," Spinella said. "What you're going to hear now may be the ending you are hoping for, Mrs. Evans."

****

Jack O'Neil came in.

"I really apologize to all of you. There were some details about Newman I had to take care of today."

"Jack, can you pick up the story from when John was in Boys Republic?"

"Did you know Newman when he was in that place?" Danny asked.

"No, Danny. I met John, or Newman, shortly after he got out," O'Neill said.

Danny was getting more than a little agitated.

"Listen, Newman or Peralta, whichever it is, I want to know why!" he demanded.

O'Neil and Spinella looked at each other as if to say, "Who's going to tell them?" Spinella spoke first.

"While John was in Boys Republic, he met a priest who addressed a group of the boys when they were about a year away from release. John was one of them. He told them he knew a way to guarantee they would never come back. All they had to do was come and talk to him. Well, John did. The priest told him every day when you get up, you must decide to be a better man than you were the day before. You must commit to doing something good for a stranger, to care a little more about things you love than you did the day before. In effect, the priest told John to become a new man with every day."

Danny looked across the table at the attorney. "It can't be that simple," he said. "New man became Newman?"

"Yeah, it was that simple," said O'Neill. "I thought the same when I first heard his story."

O'Neill looked at Bill Evans, "Here's the good part you are looking for. In late 1952 John Peralta showed up at my surf shop in Santa Cruz, looking for a job. He was willing to sweep floors or anything to make a few dollars. Only problem was, he told me about the Boys Republic. Well, I gave him an application. When I looked at it, he put his first initial as 'A' and his last name as Newman. He told me a family attorney had helped him make it his legal name."

Debbie Evans began to smile. "Your father, Mr. Spinella?"

"Guilty as charged," grinned the attorney.

O'Neill continued. "In 1953 I developed a process to make wetsuits out of a substance called neoprene. The problem was I didn't have much of a marketing plan. I was just going to sell them out of a couple of surfboard shops I ran at the time. Well, John, now Newman, came to me with an idea. Why not develop a mail catalog with colors, sizes, customized logos, and mail them to every known surf shop, dive shop, water rescue organization, etc. in the United States? At the time, I ran a real "mom and pop" operation. I had two shops, one in San Francisco and one in Santa Cruz. When Newman agreed to handle the wet suits sales if he could be paid on commission, I jumped at the chance. Over the next 15 years Newman made himself and me millionaires."

"In all the years I've known him, I never knew Newman to have two nickels to rub together," Father Mike said. "Though I have to admit I was curious when they got his check for your tuition at Holy Cross, Danny."

"Newman did that?" Debbie asked.

"Yes, and more," the attorney said. "He made up for the $100,000.00 commitment Wilson Collison reneged on when he withdrew his son, Garrett, from Holy Cross. His $500,000.00 donation to Burke preparatory, specifically for minority scholarships, paved the way for countless kids like Beni Andrews. It was well known in any of Jack's stores, if a kid came in and told someone he was saving his pennies to buy a surfboard by O'Neill, the store would make the sale and then charge Newman's account."

They sat in silence marveling at the generosity of the man they knew as Newman. Anthony Spinella had processed hundreds of estates. This was the first one where no one asked who was getting what. They were in for a surprise. Finally, Spinella spoke.

"This is Newman's last request. He wanted his estate divided equally between all of you. Father Mike, Newman loved your sense of spirituality. Fred, he was so proud of you when you went into education to make a difference. Debbie, Newman had a special place in his heart for you and Danny. I think he saw himself in you and Danny. Lastly, Angela, Newman was so thankful for the time you two spent together and the way you let him ramble on the he did. He wanted to make things a little easier for you and your son. In typical Newman style then, these are for you."

Spinella passed each one of them an envelope. It was a letter detailing that a savings account had been established at the Bank of America in the amount of $350,000.00 for each.

****

Chapter 21

"Are you ready for this?" O'Neill asked Danny, as they attached their leash lines to their ankles.

"No," Danny said, as he slowly turned the plastic bottle attached to a rubber bracelet on his right hand. "But when it comes to the ocean and surfing, I've learned to trust what Newman said. Hell, when it comes to life, I've learned to trust him. If this is what he wants, then so be it."

One would have guessed this was exactly what Newman would want. To have his ashes sprinkled in the ocean on a perfect surf day off Pleasure Point.

Jack O'Neil had followed the weather, the cycle of the moon, the tides and then picked the day. Father Mike, Fred Wyckoff, Bill and Debbie Evans, and Angela Stevens and her 10-year-old son, Mikey, were lined along the handrail near the O'Neil house. They watched as O'Neill and Danny sat outside the break waiting for the perfect wave. Finally, O'Neill signaled to Danny. It didn't look like that big of a wave at first, but by the time the whitewater had started to curl it was the most perfect wave anyone had ever seen.

Danny took the wave. As soon as he got to his feet, he took the plastic bottle from around his wrist, flipped off the top and begin to sprinkle Newman's ashes as he rode the length of the way.

It was more than they could handle. Debbie Evans sobbed uncontrollably in her husband's arms. Father Mike's Adam's apple bobbed noticeably as he tried to control his emotions while reciting the Our Father. Fred Wyckoff made a silent vow: he would try to be as good a teacher, as good a mentor as Newman. When Danny met O'Neill at the shoreline he said, "He would've loved that one." O'Neill smiled in acknowledgment.
There was one last silent acknowledgment to Newman, and Danny and O'Neill headed up the stairs to join their friends.

****

"That's the end of a legend," O'Neill said of his good friend.

"Who's a legend, Mommy?" Angela's son asked.

"Mr. Newman was" Angela replied. "He was famous for teaching people how to surf."

"Can you teach me to surf, Mommy?" The boy pleaded.

"Honey, I don't know anything about surfing."

It was Debbie Evans who came to the boy's rescue.

211

"Mikey, my son, Danny, is a really good surfer. I'm sure he'd love to teach you how to surf."

"We couldn't possibly impose on Danny's time for something like that, Mrs. Evans," Angela said.

"Well, why don't we let Danny decide," Debbie said with a tone which implied *I know my son.*

Danny pulled the cap to his wetsuit back and knelt down on one knee. "I'd be glad to teach you how to surf, Mikey."

A glow spread over the boy's face as he turned to his mother, "Can I, can I?" he begged.

Sensing an argument would be futile, Angela caved into her son's request. "If Officer Archer has the time, I guess the answer is yes."

The boy turned to Archer who was still on one knee.

"When can we start, Officer Archer?"

Danny put his arms over his knee. "When the time is right, Mikey."

That wonderful smile of childhood anticipation at the thought of getting surfing lessons immediately vanished from the boy's face. Archer might as well have answered the boy in Greek.

"I don't understand," the boy replied with the slightest tone of a whimper in his voice.

"I know, Mikey, and neither did I when I asked Newman the same question. Here's what I mean. When your homework is done and all the chores your mother needs help with around the house are done, that's when the time is right."

Danny stood up and asked Angela, "Do you have a pen and piece of paper?"

Angela opened her purse and gave Danny one of her business cards and a pen. Archer wrote his name and number on the back and gave it to the boy.

"Call me when you're ready."

A radiant smile returned to the boy's face.

"You know, Jack," Father Mike said. "I think his legend lives on."

****

Made in the USA
Las Vegas, NV
01 April 2022

46716415R00125